USBORNE

SANDY
LANE
STABLES

RIDE BY MOONLIGHT

Michelle Bates

First published in 1997 by Usborne Publishing Ltd, Usborne House, 83-85 Saffron Hill, London EC1N 8RT, England.

ISBN 0 7460 2480 0 (paperback)

ISBN 0 7460 2481 9 (hardback)

Typeset in Times

Printed and bound in Great Britain by

Biddles Ltd, Guildford and King's Lynn

Editor: Susannah Leigh
Series Editor: Gaby Waters
Designer: Lucy Parris
Cover photograph supplied by: Bob Langrish
Map illustrations by John Woodcock

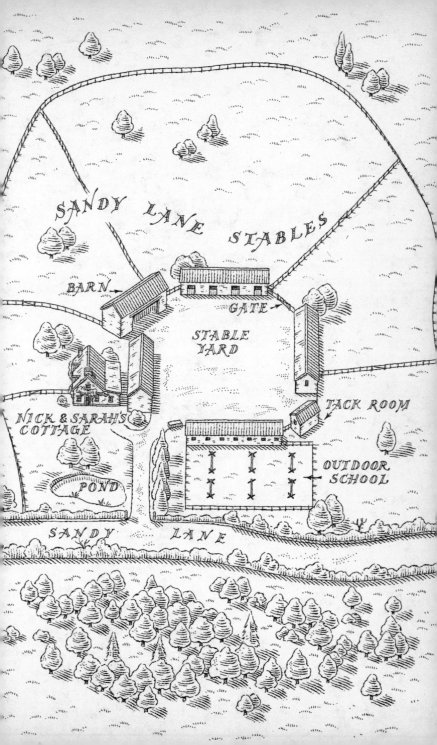

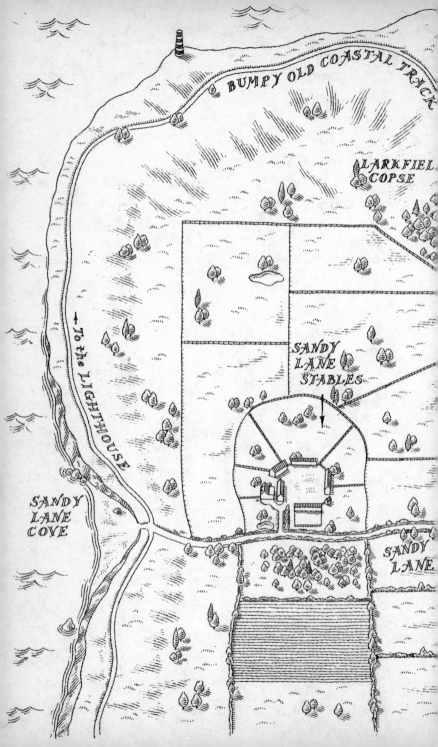

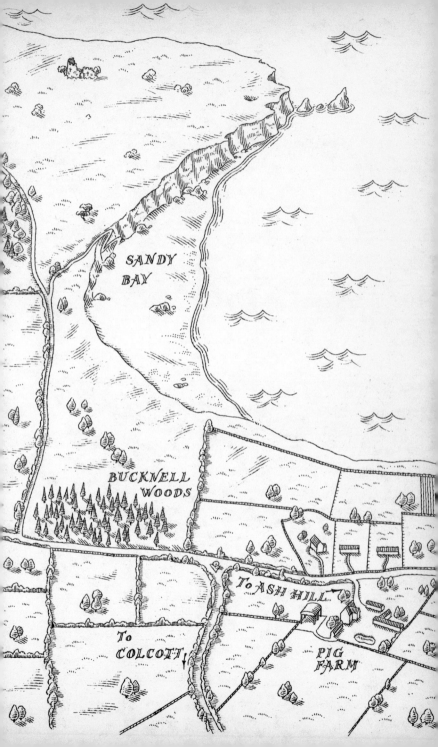

SANDY
BAY

BUCKNELL
WOODS

To ASH HILL

To
COLCOTT

PIG
FARM

CONTENTS

1

HEATED WORDS

"I can't Tom... and that's the end of it. I'm not riding again!" Charlie Marshall looked up from where he was grooming the piebald pony at Sandy Lane Stables, his green eyes flashing angrily. "Just get out of my face," he shouted. "It's got nothing to do with you. I'm not stopping you from riding, and at least it'll be less competition for you as the star rider here."

"That's not fair," Tom started.

Charlie didn't answer, but just furiously went back to what he was doing. Tom shrugged his shoulders and left him to it. Charlie felt bad as he leaned out over the stable door and watched him go. Tom was a good friend, and he hadn't meant things to turn into a blazing row, but right now the subject of riding was a very touchy one.

Charlie thought about calling Tom back over and apologizing, but something stopped him. A little nagging voice in his head told him it would only make things worse – that Tom would only think he'd given in, and things would just flare up again. Charlie didn't want that. Nothing anyone could do, nothing anyone could say, was going to make him change his mind. He wasn't getting back into the saddle, and that was that. It was only the second week of the summer holidays too – whatever was he going to do with his time if he wasn't riding?

Charlie sighed. More than anything, he'd have liked to forget the accident he'd had at the Elmwood Racing Stables last week, but he couldn't. He couldn't forget it. He looked at his watch. Five past eleven. On any normal Tuesday he'd have been racing on the gallops there by now. He'd been riding out two mornings a week and hadn't missed a slot since May. Even in term time he'd still managed to get there before school, and it was a good hour's bus ride away. But since the accident, he hadn't felt like going back. He'd been phoning in sick, hiding out at his usual stables – Sandy Lane.

Charlie had been riding at Sandy Lane Stables for over two years now – ever since his parents had divorced – and he'd fitted in almost immediately. He'd got on really well with all the regular riders, and the owners of the stables, Nick and Sarah Brooks, couldn't have been more friendly. In fact, it was Nick who first

suggested Charlie think about a future as a jockey...
Nick who convinced him he'd got the talent. He was
the right size for it too, for Charlie was small for his
age.

Once the idea had been put into Charlie's head,
there had been no stopping him. He'd got a place at
the British Racing School for September on the
understanding that he came with four months race
work experience, and that had been easy enough to
arrange. Josh Wiley, the racehorse trainer at Elmwood,
had been advertising for someone to ride out for him
for the summer. It had all fallen into place – almost as
though it was fated.

"Hey Charlie, are you OK?" Jess Adams's cheery
face peered over the stable door at him.

"I'm fine," he answered abruptly.

"You're very quiet in there," she laughed, tying her
messy, brown curls into a ponytail.

"Just thinking," he grunted. "About the accident and
stuff."

"Oh." Jess didn't know what to say. "I'm going to
my jumping lesson," she muttered, and quickly
disappeared off to Skylark's stable.

Charlie shrugged his shoulders. For the last week
his friends had been trying to get him back on a horse,
and now that it was clear that they wouldn't be able
to, they seemed at a loss to know what to do. Rosie
and Jess went on as though nothing had happened;
Kate and her brother Alex avoided the subject; and
Izzy – well, even Izzy seemed too busy with her horse,

3

Midnight, to talk about it. Charlie knew they probably just didn't know what to say, but it didn't make him feel very good. Perhaps he just needed a break from horses. Maybe he just needed to get away from it all. But how? How could he get away from it all when he was living at Sandy Lane for the summer?

It had seemed such a good idea back in May when he'd arranged to board at the stables for the holidays. His mother was going to Florida with her new boyfriend, Jeff, and had wanted Charlie to go with them. But that would have meant giving up everything – his race training, the Colcott Show, the August Bank Holiday Show. Staying with Nick and Sarah at the cottage had seemed like the perfect solution. And, as Sarah was pregnant, Nick needed some extra help. Charlie's mother had readily agreed to it. She wasn't bad like that. Charlie knew that she sometimes found it difficult to understand him, but she supported him all the way with his riding.

Charlie led Pepper out of his stable and held his head while the rider mounted. Nick was taking a training session in the outdoor school right now. With all of the summer shows coming up, excitement was high. But as Pepper plodded off to join the back of the string of horses, Charlie felt only relief that he wasn't taking part. He looked around him. The yard was almost empty. It was a hot July day, but Charlie felt unnaturally cold. He shivered as images of the accident invaded his thoughts. He closed his eyes... the horse walked through the gate... the grass fell away and they stretched out into a gallop. The trees flashed past in a whirl of green. Pounding hooves rang in Charlie's ears and a lurching, sickening feeling spiralled around his stomach. The horse collapsed into nothing and...

"Charlie, Charlie. Are you listening to me?"

Charlie was brought back to earth with a bump by the sound of Tom's voice echoing around the yard.

"What? Oh yes, I'm listening," he answered.

"Good. Well, come on then," Tom urged.

"What?" Charlie looked puzzled.

"Didn't you hear a word I was saying?" Tom tried again. "Go and tack up Napoleon. Let's go out for a ride. Come on, it'll be fine."

Tom was the only one who hadn't stopped hassling Charlie. His voice was coaxing, but Charlie couldn't help feeling irritated.

"Look," he said, grimly. "Just let it rest, will you? I've told you I'm not riding."

And with that Charlie walked away. If Tom thought it would be that easy to change his mind then Tom clearly didn't understand how difficult things were for him. But then how could he expect his friend to understand? How could he expect any of them to appreciate what he'd gone through when he hadn't told them the full story of what had happened at the racing stables?

All was quiet as Charlie wandered off down the driveway. He stopped by the outdoor school and watched as Kate positioned Feather at the wall and neatly popped over. The rest of his friends were there – Alex, Izzy, Rosie and Jess – all of the regular riders were practising hard. But not Tom. He really ought to go and look for his friend and apologize.

Quickly, Charlie strode back up the drive and made the rounds of the boxes. He found Tom in Chancey's stable, picking out one of his horse's hooves.

"Er, Tom." Charlie spoke gruffly, digging his hands deep into his pockets.

Tom looked up, startled, causing Chancey to edge away.

"What is it now?" he asked crossly.

"Look, I'm sorry about earlier," Charlie started.

"That's OK." Tom shrugged, but Charlie could tell by his brusque manner that his feelings had been hurt. "I'm glad you've seen sense. Go and get Napoleon and we'll go out. Let's forget what was said."

Charlie felt that Tom was pushing him now. Firmly, he looked Tom in the eye. "I can't," he said, trying to keep his cool. "I'm not ready. Look," he tried again. "Why don't we take the afternoon off – go down to the swimming pool or something. What do you say?"

"Some other time, Charlie," Tom answered him abruptly. "I've got to train Chancey this afternoon. We need to practise if we're going to be ready in time for the Colcott Show next week, and you ought to be doing the same, you know."

"I've told you – the last thing I feel like doing at the moment is riding," Charlie said, the anger rising in his throat in spite of himself. "And if you can't understand

6

that then– "

"Then what?" Tom challenged him.

"Forget it." Charlie thrust his hands deep into his pockets and stared into the distance.

"Look Charlie," Tom said, more kindly this time. "You've got to pull yourself together. You've had a whole week to get back on a horse and you still haven't done anything about it. Everyone's losing patience with you."

"Oh yeah?" Charlie shouted. "Like who?"

"Like Nick... like Sarah, like just about all of us at Sandy Lane," Tom said. "I know you had a nasty fall, but it's not as though you broke any bones or anything. Get back on a horse and get over it. Stop feeling sorry for yourself."

Charlie looked ready to explode. "Stop feeling sorry for myself? Who do you think you are?"

Tom shrugged his shoulders. "I'm not trying to wind you up," he said quickly. "But if you're not riding soon, Josh Wiley will find someone else to ride out for him and you won't get into racing school without the experience. I can't sit by and watch you throw your place away like some loser."

Charlie looked at Tom in disbelief. He was proud. He'd tried to apologize, and it had been thrown back in his face. Without another word, he turned on his heels and disappeared across the yard in the direction of Nick and Sarah's cottage. Marching into the kitchen, Charlie slammed the back door shut behind him. Once alone inside, he stood with his back to the door and let out a huge sigh. And now his whole brave facade collapsed. He was so tired... tired of all the lies he was telling. And to top it all, he had a bad headache, a dull ache right behind his eyes.

A nasty fall, Tom had called it. If only he knew the horrible truth. Let them all think he was a loser – that was just punishment for what he'd done.

Charlie walked into the hallway, knocking the black labrador, Ebony, out of the way as he passed. Ebony yelped and looked up at him reproachfully.

"I'm sorry. I'm so sorry." Charlie knelt down to pat the dog's head. "I didn't mean to take it out on you."

2

THE NIGHTMARE

Charlie tossed and turned in his sleep. The rhythmic drumming of horses' hooves throbbed in his head as he leaned forward in the saddle. On and on he galloped, the wind biting into his face. The ground dropped away as the other horses rode past. Charlie felt a sense of urgency rising in his throat, almost choking him, as he shielded himself from the mud spray. One more crack from the whip... one more nudge from his heels. Nearer and nearer they flew, closer to the spot.

"Stop, stop!" he cried now. But every tug on the reins seemed to send the racehorse faster and faster, until Charlie's head was reeling. Furiously, they raced across the turf to the brow of the hill. Just over the top and down the side. Charlie's heart was in his mouth. He knew what was coming next, and yet he couldn't stop it. Closer and closer, nearly there now.

And then, suddenly, the black thoroughbred was dropping away, falling... falling... falling. The glint of the horses' racing plates ahead of him was all that Charlie saw as he hit the ground, tucking himself into a neat ball as he rolled, over and over... *You little idiot... you silly fool... you must have been riding too fast... of course it was your fault...*

Charlie sat up rigid, the words echoing in his ears. His bedclothes were wringing wet; his heart was banging away. It was a dream, just a dream, he told himself, the same dream he'd been having for a week now.

He looked at his watch. No point in trying to get back to sleep – he'd told Nick he'd help him bring in the horses at seven thirty.

Throwing back the duvet, Charlie jumped out of bed and struggled into his clothes. Quickly, he made his way down the stairs to the kitchen. Sarah was already up and, as Charlie walked into the kitchen, she looked surprised to see him.

"Oh Charlie, you made me jump," she said.

"I couldn't sleep I– I–" Charlie didn't know what to say.

"Is there anything you'd like to talk about?" Sarah suggested.

Charlie hesitated. "I don't know I–" Charlie stopped himself. Hadn't Tom already told him that everyone

10

was losing patience with him? Sarah had enough on her plate with a baby on the way, without being burdened with his problems too. Yet Charlie desperately needed to talk to someone.

"Come on," Sarah urged. "I couldn't sleep either. The baby's been kicking all night," she said, patting her huge belly.

"OK, well thanks." Charlie sat down at the round oak table as Sarah filled the teapot.

"Just over a month to go now," she said, laughing as she dumped two cups of tea on the table and eased herself down onto the chair. "I'll be so glad to be a normal size again." Sarah was nearly eight months pregnant and it really showed. She took off her tortoiseshell glasses and rubbed her eyes. "Why don't you start at the beginning. And don't worry about boring me. I'm happy to listen if it will stop you from mooching around the yard as if the world's come to an end."

"If it's going to be another lecture, then I don't want to hear it," Charlie said, defensively. "Tom's already gone on at me enough about it."

"No, it's not a lecture," Sarah said. "I'm not going to talk. You are."

"Well." Charlie stared across the room to where the morning light was streaming in through the windows. Sarah followed his gaze and got up from the table. She pulled back the curtains, so they could see out onto the yard, and sat back down. "I wish it was as simple as everyone seems to think," Charlie started. "I wish it *was* just a case of getting back on a horse. Only I can't seem to get the accident out of my head. I suppose at first I thought it was like all the other times I'd fallen, and you know there have been enough of those," he laughed nervously. "Only this time it's different. The feeling I had – well it was like nothing I've ever felt before." He was trying to explain things, but he knew he was waffling.

Sarah looked at him. "Go on," she said.

"I thought I was all right at first," he started again. "It was only when I got back to the racing stables after the ride that I realized I wasn't, that I'd been scared. It's like the feeling you get on a roller coaster – you go up and down and upside down, and all the time your heart is in your mouth. You're wondering what's coming next, and yet you know you're safe because it's all programmed. It's not like that when you're riding. When you're riding, you're the one in control."

"You've been thinking about this too much," Sarah said, gently.

"I know, I know," Charlie said, holding his head in his hands.

Sarah looked across at Charlie. His blond hair flopped forward, masking his face, making it hard for her to read anything in his expression.

"I think I can understand what you're going through," she said, soothingly. "And you're right – when you're riding, you are the one in charge, which is why you have to be completely sure about what

12

you're doing. That shouldn't scare you. Josh Wiley wouldn't have taken you on if he didn't think you were up to it, and you know Nick has complete confidence in your riding."

Charlie looked up. His face was pale and drawn, his mouth pinched and thin.

"You'll find a lot of people go through this at some point in their riding careers," Sarah went on. "Lots of riders have falls... falls that scare them... terrify them even. But a true horseman doesn't give in – you *must* ride again." Sarah sat quietly, waiting for a response, and when it didn't come, she leaned forward. "Look Charlie," she started. "Is there something you're not telling us?"

Charlie gulped. This was the perfect opportunity to get everything off his chest. Sarah would understand, wouldn't she?

"I know it's been hard for you since the divorce," Sarah started again. "And it must be difficult seeing your mother with someone else, but you've got to start to rebuild your life now. She'll be back from Florida soon and then things will be back to normal. She's not away for long. It'll be all right."

Charlie didn't know what to think. Sarah had totally misread his discomfort if she thought he was still worried about his parents' divorce – that was the last thing on his mind. He felt like screaming out in frustration. Instead, he spoke in a calm and reasonable manner.

"Nick thinks I'm making a mountain out of a

molehill, doesn't he?" he said.

"No," Sarah said, hesitantly. "It's just that he can't understand why you're not riding again. "He tried everything to get you on Napoleon last week, and when he couldn't manage it, it made him feel frustrated."

Charlie didn't know what to say.

"Now listen, I think that's him moving about upstairs," Sarah said. "Let's wrap this up while I make some more tea." And, getting up from her seat, Sarah flicked the kettle on.

"Hello everyone. What's going on here?" Before Charlie knew it, Nick appeared in the kitchen and sat himself down at the table. "Any news?" he asked, running a hand through his ruffled brown hair. "You going over to the racing stables this morning then, Charlie?" he interjected, casually.

"Nick," Sarah said pleadingly, shooting him a look that clearly asked him to be quiet. Nick held up his hand to silence her, waiting for Charlie's response.

"No," Charlie said, obstinately.

"And why not?" Nick asked.

"You know why not," Sarah said, intervening on Charlie's behalf.

"Look Nick," Charlie said in a defensive voice. "I told Josh I'd let him know when I'm going back." Charlie felt guilty, knowing that he wasn't telling Nick the whole truth.

"You said that last week, Charlie," Nick said, more gently this time.

14

"Does it matter?" Charlie raised his voice.

"Yes, it does. You should be trying to ride again." Nick's voice was calmly controlled.

Charlie bit his tongue. And then he started to speak. "I've told you," he said, brusquely. "I'm not up to it yet." And with that he got up and walked out of the kitchen, slamming the door behind him. As he stepped into the hall, he stopped for a second and took a deep breath. He ought to go back and apologize. But now he could hear Sarah and Nick talking again.

"Honestly Nick," Sarah was saying. "It's not as simple as you think. It's important we give him time to come to terms with everything. You of all people should understand that."

"And what's that supposed to mean?" Nick answered, crossly.

"Do I need to spell it out for you?" Sarah answered. "You know what I'm referring to."

"And you know I don't like talking about my old racing days. We're not discussing me here." Nick raised his voice. "It's Charlie we've got to think about. He really should be pulling himself together."

Charlie stood still in the hall, rooted to the spot. At the sound of the kitchen door beginning to open, he made a quick exit up the stairs. He'd heard enough. Nick and Sarah never normally argued and now, because of him, they were angry with each other.

Quickly, Charlie closed the bedroom door behind

him. He couldn't keep disrupting everything. He'd just have to work out a way to get himself riding again, or give up Sandy Lane altogether.

3

ANOTHER TRY

As Sandy Lane was right by the sea, it was the perfect place to ride in the summer months, and that morning the yard was flooded with extra riders. Charlie found himself running around, grooming, tacking up and taking bookings. It wasn't until 11 o'clock that he found time for a rest, and sat down on the hay bales by the big barn.

"Jess, do you want a hand with Skylark?" he called across to where the curly-haired girl was struggling to pull her pony's head up from the grass.

"No, I'm all right, Charlie," she called back, fumbling with the girth.

"OK," Charlie answered. He longed for everyone to be ready so that the yard would be quiet again.

Eventually everything seemed to be in hand – the

ponies were tacked up, the riders mounted, and a string of horses made its way out of the yard. Charlie breathed a sigh of relief as he watched the retreating figures.

As the morning sun bore down on him, Charlie looked across to where Chancey was kept. His stable door stood open. Tom was probably inside, but Tom had ignored him all morning. In fact, they hadn't talked since their argument. Charlie was in a quandary. He'd made up his mind to try to ride, and he wanted to ask Tom for help. But that would mean apologizing for yesterday's argument, and he really didn't want to do that.

He looked at his watch. Ten past eleven. The ride wouldn't be back for a good hour and a half – just enough time to take a horse out. It was now or never. He'd just have to say sorry. Slowly, Charlie eased himself off the hay bales.

"Tom," he called.

No answer. Tom clearly wasn't going to make things easy for him. Charlie took a deep breath and crossed the yard.

He called again and peered into the gloom of Chancey's stable to find Tom, frantically brushing away at the chestnut horse's tail.

"What is it?" Tom asked, brushing the hair out of his eyes as he squinted into the brilliant sunshine outside. "I thought you'd said all you wanted to say yesterday."

"Look, I know you're mad at me," Charlie began,

18

"but I've changed my mind. I do want to try and ride again."

"So what?" Tom looked angrily at Charlie. He seemed more annoyed than pleased by the news. It wasn't the reaction Charlie had been expecting.

"Well, can we go out for that ride you promised me yesterday?" Charlie asked, trying to make light of the situation.

"You've got a cheek, haven't you? Just changing your mind like that," Tom answered him.

"I know, it doesn't sound great," Charlie said, biting his tongue to stop a smart retort. If he was going to get Tom on his side, he'd have to be as conciliatory as possible. "But you were right. I've got to try and pull myself together."

Tom looked uncertain. "Well, I'm taking Chancey down to the beach for a good hard gallop to muscle him up. I suppose you can come too if you like," he said grudgingly.

Charlie gulped. A good hard gallop was the last thing he felt like. But Tom hadn't stopped for a reply.

"Nick's just gone out," he went on. "So you'd better ask Sarah if you can take out Napoleon."

"But Tom, I'm not sure if–" Charlie started.

Tom held up his hand. "I'm sure she'll let you."

"OK." Charlie was hesitant. He'd wanted to tell Tom that he was suddenly getting cold feet again, but Tom had interrupted him.

"Go on then," Tom started.

Charlie felt beads of sweat rising on his forehead

as he hurried across to the cottage. He felt embarrassed as he walked into the kitchen. He'd only been saying to Sarah that morning that he wouldn't ride. What would she say?

Sarah was quietly composed as Charlie made his request. "Are you sure about this?" she asked. "Tom hasn't put you up to it, has he?"

"No, it's completely my decision," Charlie answered firmly.

"Well, OK then." She seemed surprised. "If you're sure you're ready for it, then of course it's fine for you to take out Napoleon. You're a competent rider. Nick won't have a problem with that. It's just that after everything you said this morning—"

"I know, I know," Charlie answered, cutting her off mid-sentence.

"Well that's settled then. I won't say anything more about it. I'll see you later."

Charlie nodded and tried to force a smile to his face.

"All agreed?" Tom asked as he saw Charlie approaching. Charlie nodded.

"Good, well I'll get Chancey ready and then we'll be off."

Tom disappeared, leaving Charlie to tack up his mount. Charlie made his way to Napoleon's stable.

"You've got to help me through this," Charlie said to the big, bay horse. "I'm relying on you to look after me."

Napoleon looked around him and blew through his nostrils in a bored fashion.

"It's all right for you," Charlie said, reaching for the saddle and bridle. The stable felt oppressively hot and still, and Charlie had an empty, gnawing feeling in the pit of his stomach.

"There's a boy," he whispered, gently sliding the bridle over Napoleon's head. He reached up to place the saddle on the horse's back and pulled the girth round. As he fastened the buckle, he realized he was shaking. He stood up straight, stopping for a moment to fiddle with Napoleon's forelock – anything to prolong the moment when he'd have to go out of the stable and mount.

"It'll be all right. It'll be all right," he tried telling himself and then, in a daze, he led Napoleon out of the stable. Before he could change his mind, he was following Tom out of the yard, through the gate and into the dusty fields at the back of the yard. He felt giddy as he watched Tom spring neatly into Chancey's saddle.

"Come on. Let's get going," Tom said firmly.

"I think I'll just walk Napoleon over to the trees," Charlie said, playing for time. "It'll be easier over there."

"OK." Tom was adjusting his stirrup, and seemed not to notice Charlie's discomfort.

Charlie didn't know why he felt so ill at ease. He'd ridden Napoleon so many times. He didn't even bear any similarity to the racehorse. Big, solid, reliable Napoleon – how could he be scared of riding him? And yet he was.

Napoleon seemed to sense that something was wrong now they had crossed the field. He was getting fidgety, turning on his toes and pirouetting madly, making it difficult for Charlie to get his foot into the stirrup. Every time Charlie went to spring up, Napoleon moved away again. The ground started spinning. Charlie's head was reeling. It was as though he was seeing everything double. He felt dizzy and suddenly very numb. He couldn't think. He couldn't stop thinking. His mind was in a whirl as everything came flooding back – the high-pitched whinny, the thundering hooves, the crashing fall – they all echoed around his head.

Charlie had an overwhelming feeling that he was going to be sick as he leaned against the horse. He felt like he wasn't really there, and yet he could hear Tom calling his name.

"Charlie, are you OK? You've gone very green." Tom's voice snapped him to his senses.

"Er, I'm OK, I just don't feel too good. Look, I don't think I should come out with you today after all."

Charlie felt groggy as he reached up to touch his forehead. "I'm just tired. I didn't sleep last night. It must all be beginning to catch up with me."

"Tired! You're more than tired," said Tom. "Let's go and get Sarah."

"No, no, don't do that," Charlie said hurriedly. "I'm starting to feel better already. Only I really don't think I should ride Napoleon this morning."

"You're probably right," Tom said, uneasily.

"Look, you won't tell anyone about this, will you?" Charlie pleaded, embarrassed.

"Well..." Tom was hesitant.

"Please," Charlie begged. "I just need more time. I'm not feeling quite myself at the moment, that's all. I'll be better in a few days – honest I will. You go out for your ride. Chancey's getting impatient. I'll take Napoleon back, and we'll go out another time."

"I really think I ought to come with you," Tom said, uncertainly.

"No, Tom," Charlie said, more firmly this time. "No offence, but I'll be fine on my own."

"OK then," Tom said, slowly. "Look, I'll only be gone half an hour."

"I'll see you later," Charlie answered, wearily.

And, before Tom could say anything more about it, Charlie was leading the bay horse off by his reins.

As he walked back to the yard, Charlie felt ashamed of himself. How could he have been such a wimp? As he took Napoleon into the stable, he felt relieved to see that the Land Rover had gone – Sarah must be shopping. At least she wouldn't have to know about this.

Leaving Napoleon to his haynet, Charlie hurried over to the cottage. He fumbled under the mat for the key and let himself into the kitchen. Sarah had drawn all of the curtains so that it was kept cool inside – a dramatic contrast to the burning heat of the yard. And now that he was alone, Charlie reached for the phone, gnawing at his lip as he punched in some numbers, before collapsing into the armchair behind him.

"Hello, this is Charlie Marshall speaking... er no, no, I don't need Mr. Wiley. Yes, please could you just tell him that I won't be over this week... er no, I don't feel great. It's summer 'flu. Yes, a lot of it around. Thanks very much."

4

MORE LIES

Charlie was still slumped in the chair when he heard the Land Rover roll into the yard an hour later. The others had got back from their hack some time ago, but Charlie had stayed well hidden... hadn't answered any of their calls, not even Tom's. He'd just wanted to be left alone. Now that Sarah was back, he'd have to go outside, or at least disappear up to his room, if he was going to avoid facing her.

Charlie pushed open the back door and stepped outside. His friends were huddled over in a group by the hay bales, but they were so busy talking they didn't seem to notice him lingering by the barn.

"I just don't know what's wrong with Izzy," Rosie was saying.

"She's been like a bear with a sore head lately,"

Jess added. "Yesterday I offered to help her with Midnight, and she practically bit my head off – told me he was her horse, not mine – as if I didn't know that."

"Something's definitely wrong," Kate joined in. "I just can't work out what it is."

Charlie felt guilty as he listened to what they were saying. He'd been so wrapped up with his own problems that he hadn't noticed the things going on around him.

"Oh, Charlie, there you are," Rosie and Jess called out in unison. "We've been calling and calling you. Where have you been? Didn't you hear us?"

"Er, no," Charlie said hesitantly. "What's all this about Izzy?" he asked, quickly changing the subject before they could question him more.

"Oh, it's just that she's been really odd lately. We're sure something's up, only she won't tell us. Do you know what's wrong?"

Charlie shook his head. He thought about Izzy. She'd always been headstrong, but she was never moody for long. She'd been strange with him lately too, but Charlie had put it down to embarrassment about his accident.

"Hi you guys." The group turned round to see the very person they were discussing crossing the yard to join them. Quickly, they broke up the group, feeling embarrassed that they'd actually been caught talking about her behind her back. An unnatural silence developed that was only broken when Tom joined the group. Once again, the focus turned back to Charlie.

"Where have you been?" Tom asked, walking over. "I've been searching everywhere for you, Charlie. Didn't you hear me calling?"

"No," Charlie said, avoiding eye contact and turning away.

"Are you lot OK over there?" Nick interrupted the group. "If any of you are joining the 2 o'clock hack you'd better get a move on – it's about to go out."

Uneasily, Charlie shifted his weight from one foot to the other, hoping that Nick wouldn't suggest he join the ride. Luckily for him though, Nick seemed to have other things on his mind, and then Sarah appeared at the steps to the cottage.

"Can someone help me in with the shopping?" she called.

"I will," Charlie answered, quick to jump to help.

"So will I," Tom added.

"Great! So how did the ride go then you two?" she asked brightly, looking straight at Tom and Charlie.

"What ride?" Nick asked, suspiciously.

Sarah shrugged her shoulders and went to speak. "Well–"

And then Charlie stepped in. Before he could stop himself, more lies were spilling out.

"Tom took Chancey out for a training session in the outdoor school and I went and watched," he explained. "You're not going to believe it, but they jumped four foot!" Charlie looked Tom straight in the eye, challenging him to defy him. Tom watched him warily, but didn't say anything.

"Four foot?" Nick looked from Tom to Charlie as if they were mad. "But Chancey easily jumped that last summer. You'll have to do better than that if you're going to impress me," he laughed. "He's a brilliant horse, he should be jumping four footers easily."

"I know, I know," Tom laughed, uneasily. "I did try telling Charlie that, but he wouldn't have it."

Sarah looked bemused, but didn't say anything. "Well, anyway – the shopping," she started, quickly changing the subject. "Tom and Charlie. Can you carry the bags in?"

"Do you want me to give you a hand too?" Nick asked.

"No thanks," Sarah answered. "Two pairs of hands is plenty. Shouldn't you be getting ready for the beach hack?"

"Yes, I guess I should." Nick shrugged his shoulders good-naturedly and turned away. When he was out of earshot, Sarah looked angrily at the two boys in front of her.

"OK you two," she said, pushing her hair behind her ears. "Inside the cottage. You might be able to pull the wool over Nick's eyes – he's got a lot on at the moment, but you won't get things past me that easily."

Obediently, Charlie and Tom picked up the bags of shopping and followed Sarah into the cottage.

"So," she started. "What's going on?"

Charlie looked at Tom. Tom looked at Charlie, and then Charlie started to speak. When he did, it wasn't the truth he came out with.

"We didn't want Nick to know I'd been riding yet. You see, I didn't do anything much – I took it very easy. Just walking and trotting. And I don't want Nick to get his hopes up if it comes to nothing."

"Still, it's a start, isn't it?" Sarah said, looking relieved. "Didn't I tell you you'd get back on a horse, Charlie?" she beamed.

"Yes," Charlie said, cringing inwardly at his deceit.

Tom was silent during this exchange.

"Well, it's brilliant news, isn't it?" she interrupted, ignoring Tom's stony face. "You can't expect miracles straight away. Good on you, Charlie. When are you going out again then?" she asked.

"Er, I'm not sure," he said, turning away. "Soon."

"Well, don't leave it too long," Sarah said. "Or you'll have undone all your good work."

"I know," Charlie said, blushing furiously. "Now, hadn't we better get the rest of the shopping in?" he asked, quickly changing the subject.

"Good idea," Sarah said. "But you really ought to tell Nick soon that you're back riding again – he's away on his advanced dressage training course next week, and I wouldn't want you to be riding all that time without him knowing. Anyway, I'll leave you to sort that out. If you can just bring in the shopping, that would be great, then I can unpack."

Charlie nodded and the two boys trooped out of the

29

cottage.

"Why on earth didn't you tell her the truth?" Tom hissed once they were out of earshot. "All that nonsense about walking and trotting. I've had enough of all this. I'm not going to keep covering up for you. You've got to tell them you're not really riding yet, or they're going to expect more and more from you."

Charlie didn't say anything.

"Look," Tom started again, more kindly this time. "Just tell them what happened – tell them how dreadful you felt with Napoleon. It's nothing to be ashamed of."

"I just want to tackle things in my own time, Tom," Charlie said gruffly. "Surely you of all people can understand that."

Tom looked unconvinced. "I know I took things slowly when I first got Chancey, but that was different. I had lots of time then. Remember, we've got the Colcott Show next week. If you haven't sorted anything out by then, you're going to have to let Nick know you're not going to be riding Napoleon."

"I know, I know," Charlie said, impatiently. "I'm sure I'll be back riding in a few days time."

Tom shrugged his shoulders and quickly turned away, leaving Charlie alone with his guilt. *'Nothing to be ashamed of'* – those had been Tom's words. If only he knew the truth. And while it was easy to *sound* confident in front of Tom, Charlie didn't feel it. He didn't feel it at all. In fact, he didn't know if he'd ever be able to put everything about the accident behind him.

5

THE PRESSURE MOUNTS

As excitement about the forthcoming Colcott Show ran high in the yard over the next few days, Charlie started to feel a little better. Soon he found himself swept away with it all, in spite of himself. It was always like that before a show – even more so because it was the first major show of the summer. It was hard not to feel some enthusiasm when it was all his friends were talking about – some taking it more seriously than others of course...

That morning, Charlie stood watching Jess and Rosie in the fields behind the yard. He couldn't help smiling at their clowning around. Both of them were entered for just about all of the gymkhana events and, fiercely competitive, they were taking everything very seriously.

"Skylark knocked that pole down. Come on, Jess, admit it," Rosie squealed.

"Rubbish," Jess laughed. "Skylark's the perfect pony, she wouldn't make a mistake like that," Jess giggled. "Charlie... Charlie, can you come here?"

And before Charlie knew it, he had been summoned over as lines judge for the two girls. Once more they tore up and down the field, swerving in and out of the standing poles, faster than a streak of lightning.

"You see, I told you Skylark's the best," Jess shouted as she crossed the line a second before Rosie.

"Well, if you look behind you, you'll see you've knocked three poles down again," Rosie said smugly.

"Bother." Jess looked puzzled.

"Instant disqualification." A voice came from behind them. Rosie and Jess turned to see Izzy arriving on the back of Midnight. "Only joking," she said. "Can I join you?"

"Of course," Rosie and Jess said in unison, feeling relieved to see their friend in better spirits.

"Don't tell me you're going in for this lark as well, Izzy," Charlie laughed.

"Course I am," Izzy answered. "We won't stand a chance in the Open Jumping against Tom, and besides, I wouldn't miss a gymkhana for the world."

Charlie smiled. The Colcott Show was renowned for its gymkhana games, and although there was an

Open Jumping event there too, it was on the other side of the showground, so you could really only enter one or the other. Most of the Sandy Lane regulars went in for the gymkhana, knowing that there would be other more varied jumping shows later on in the summer.

Charlie wondered what Tom was doing right now. One thing was for sure, he wouldn't be fooling around in the days before a show. Tom took his jumping very seriously, and that was understandable, considering he had won the Open Jumping at Colcott for the last three years. He had a lot to live up to. Still, Charlie didn't doubt he could win again.

As Charlie wandered down the drive, he could hear the gentle sound of hooves cantering around the outdoor school. He peered through the fir trees, and caught a glimpse of Tom's powerful chestnut gelding cantering easily around a figure of eight course.

Springing up onto the railings, he sat quietly watching, waiting for Tom to notice he was there. But Tom was too engrossed in his riding. Once more around the ring he rode, before he saw Charlie and drew to a halt next to him.

"Hi, how's it going?" he asked.

"Oh, not so bad," Charlie answered. "I've just been round the back, watching Jess and Rosie messing around in the fields. They're fighting out the bending race this year."

"I don't know why they don't give the Open Jumping a shot," Tom said. "They're both pretty good."

34

"The Open Jumping trophy's got your name on it, Tom, and you know it," Charlie grinned. "Anyway, I came to find you to talk about something else. I've made a decision," he started, determinedly.

"Oh yes?" Tom sounded interested, but cautious.

"I don't think I'll enter the Colcott Show after all, but I *am* going to have another go at riding when Nick's not around next week." Charlie's voice craved reassurance.

"Next week? Where's Nick going?" Tom looked puzzled, and then he remembered. "Oh, he's on that dressage course, isn't he? I'd completely forgotten – what with the show and everything." Tom circled Chancey around. "It just seems such a waste to cancel your entry for the Open Jumping when no one else is down to ride Napoleon. You're really letting Nick and Sarah down, you know. Look, I think you should come clean about a few things. Own up and tell them how rotten you felt when you went to get on Napoleon. At least let them know why you're not riding."

"I don't know," Charlie said, gloomily. "It's just–"

Chancey tossed his head impatiently.

"Let me just take him round once more, then we can talk while I'm putting him away," Tom said, trotting Chancey to stop him getting restless.

A gentle breeze flurried through the fir trees, bringing welcome relief from the sweltering heat. Charlie watched as Tom and Chancey glided easily around the course. Tom didn't show a moment's hesitation as he positioned Chancey at the parallel. The chestnut horse responded willingly to the pressure from Tom's heels, and rose confidently for the jumps. Then it was on to the triple – one... two... three... clear. Now there was only the wall... jump and touchdown.

Charlie shivered. If only it could be that easy for him. The rhythmic sound of cantering hooves sounded around the school as he sat, silently watching. To see Tom and Chancey jumping so easily only made it all the more painful for him. If only he hadn't been so ambitious, if only he hadn't set his heart on a racing career, then he too might still be riding without a care in the world, instead of sitting on the sidelines watching.

Slowly, Tom drew Chancey to a halt beside the big oak tree and jumped to the ground. "Are you sure I can't tempt you?" he said, offering the reins over.

As Tom dangled the thing Charlie wanted more than anything in the world in front of him, he felt the frustration of the last two weeks welling up. Suddenly he could contain himself no longer.

"I can't. You see there's more to all this than you think, Tom. The accident – I mean, I didn't just fall."

Tom looked serious now. "Go on," he said. "Tell me exactly what happened."

Charlie hesitated. He hadn't told anyone the full story of that morning's events. He had blocked it for so long, hoping that by not mentioning it, it would go away, that time would heal the wound. But it hadn't, and he felt the ghost of the accident coming back to haunt him again and again.

"It's a long story," he gulped. "I don't know if I can..."

"Try," Tom offered.

"Well, I was riding out on the gallops when it happened, but you know that anyway. It was no different from any other day. I was on a mare called Night Star. We'd gone through the gate and out onto the tracks... everything was fine. I cantered off in the string, and we moved off in a gallop. The other horses started to overtake us... faster and faster. We were being left behind... very behind. I can see it all so clearly," he said, his speech speeding up in his anxiety to get everything off his chest.

"I couldn't bear it, so I gave Night Star a good kick... just to wake her up, and then a bit of a tap with the crop, and suddenly we were following along nicely. One more nudge, I thought to myself. We were galloping so fast... faster... faster."

Charlie's eyes glazed over as he got carried away with the story. "And then, before I knew it, we had fallen. We were crashing to the ground. I don't know what happened really," he said, vaguely. "It's all such a blur – all I could see was this horse lying sprawled on the ground, and she wasn't moving. I didn't know what to do. None of the others had seen me fall. It was only when they came back to find out what had happened that I realized everything. You see the horse was... was dead... I killed her."

"What? You mean the horse actually DIED?"

Charlie nodded.

Tom was shocked. "I don't know what to say. I mean, why? How? What did you do to her?" he asked, the questions tumbling out one after the other in his confusion.

"I didn't do anything, Tom." Charlie was angry. "We weren't going any faster than normal – even if O'Grady said we were."

"O'Grady?" Tom looked even more puzzled. "Who's O'Grady?"

"The head lad at Elmwood Stables," Charlie murmured. "He went mad at me... told me that I was a little idiot and that I must have been riding too fast. He said it was all my fault. Night Star was his favourite horse, you see. He was really upset."

"I'm not surprised," Tom said, a worried expression on his face. This was too much for Charlie to bear, and he exploded.

"Is that all you can say? *'I'm not surprised.'* I don't know why I thought you might understand. I should have known you wouldn't be sympathetic. Can't you see what I'm going through? I feel bad enough as it is."

Tom shifted his weight uneasily from one foot to the other. "Look, I'm sorry Charlie, but I can't help my reaction. What would you say if I told you Chancey had died when I was riding him? What did Josh Wiley have to say about it?"

"I couldn't talk to him," Charlie said, a little calmer

now. "I couldn't face him. I haven't been back to the stables since. I couldn't bear to."

"Well," Tom was hesitant. "I think you should tell Nick and Sarah about this."

"No way," Charlie answered, firmly. "Not me, not you, NO ONE is telling Nick and Sarah."

Tom looked a bit taken aback by the force of Charlie's words, and he answered equally angrily.

"Look, Charlie, I don't know how to solve this for you. If you're not going to go back to Elmwood, and you're not going to tell Nick and Sarah, then I just don't know... you'll have this hanging over your head forever."

Charlie turned and walked furiously away up the drive. Briefly he turned back.

"Don't you dare tell anyone, Tom," he called. Tom stared silently back at his friend in worried disbelief. All that Charlie could do was turn away, and hope for the best.

6

SOME UNEXPECTED ADVICE

It was a stiflingly hot day as Charlie stood at the gates to the Elmwood Racing Stables. What on earth had possessed him to tell Tom what had really happened? It had done no good at all. In fact, it seemed like the worst thing he could possibly have done. How long would it be before Nick and Sarah knew... how long would it be before everyone at the yard knew his guilty secret?

Charlie stood still, silently looking into the Elmwood yard. He'd come here to talk to Josh Wiley, and yet the last thing he felt like doing was going into the stables. It was busy – horse after horse being led out from their boxes. The yard looked really professional, and owners stood around casting a critical eye over their horses. Charlie felt both drawn to the glamour of it all, and at the same time intimidated.

A clock, perched high above the reception, chimed the time. Nine o'clock. The horses would be going off to the gallops soon. In spite of himself, Charlie felt a thrill of excitement course through him. The jockeys would mount and then they would lead off.

He felt envious as he watched a boy, no older than himself, swing easily into the saddle of a beautiful grey. It was such a different world to the friendly happy-go-lucky one of Sandy Lane. He couldn't imagine ever having been a part of it.

Charlie's eyes wandered around the stables. And then he saw Josh Wiley stride across the yard, calmly calling out instructions to all of the jockeys. He was busy... very busy. Josh wouldn't have the time to talk. Charlie felt that he shouldn't have come and, before he knew it, he had convinced himself out of doing anything about it. He took a deep breath. There really wasn't enough time to catch Josh now. With a heavy sigh, he turned away and walked back out of the yard.

****

As Charlie walked back up the drive to Sandy Lane, he caught sight of Izzy leaning against Midnight's stable. She cast a lone figure just standing there. It was late afternoon, and most of the riders were in lessons. Charlie called over to attract her attention. He desperately wanted to see a friendly face, but Izzy didn't seem to want to talk to him.

As he got nearer, he realized why. She looked as though she'd been crying. Her face was dirty and smudged and she shot him a look that clearly told him she didn't want him to be there.

"Are you OK, Izzy?" he asked, ignoring the reproachful look.

"Do I look OK?" she asked through gritted teeth, fiercely wiping a sleeve across her eyes and pushing her long, brown hair back from her face. "Look, it's nothing. I'm fine, OK? What's wrong with you anyway?"

"Oh, you know, the usual – the accident and all that." Charlie stared into the distance, his eyes watering.

And then something in Izzy seemed to snap, because as Charlie turned back to her, she stood glaring at him.

"I can't believe I'm still hearing this," she said angrily. Charlie looked flabbergasted, but she didn't let him have a moment to stop her.

"You think you're the only one who's got problems, don't you? Well, why don't you take a look around you one of these days, huh?"

"What do you mean?" Charlie said.

"If you stopped wallowing in self pity, and took an interest in someone else for a change, you'd see that some of us are miserable too. Don't you realize you're being a complete pain in the neck? You fell off a horse. Well, so what?" she cried, the anger rising in her throat. "Do you ever stop to think that something might be wrong with me, for instance?"

"So, tell me what could be wrong with you?" Charlie said in a sarcastic voice, and Izzy let it all spill out.

"Oh, only that I've just got five weeks left with Midnight, that's all, and then I go... yes, I got into boarding school, if any of you had cared to ask. I got my place at Whitecote."

"But I thought you wanted to go to boarding school, Izzy. It was all you talked about last year." So this was the reason Izzy had been so odd, and he'd thought it was because of him.

"I do want to go," Izzy answered. "It's a fantastic school, it's just it seemed so far off when I sat the entrance exam. I just didn't realize what I'd feel like having to leave Midnight behind," she said, gloomily. "Anyway, I've said enough. Obviously your life is far more important than mine," she said sarcastically. "I can't believe how everyone's pandering to you. It makes me sick. I mean you only fell, it's not as though the horse died or anything, is it?"

Charlie visibly paled. He opened his mouth to say something, and closed it again.

"Oh golly, that's it, isn't it?" Izzy's voice dropped an octave as suddenly everything dawned on her. "The horse died, didn't it?"

Charlie didn't say anything.

"Oh Charlie, how can I have been so thoughtless?" Izzy went on. "I mean... it's just... oh no, I didn't think for a moment. Oh, I'm so sorry, Charlie. I'm such a silly idiot. You must hate me," she said. "I didn't mean any of the things I said. It's just that I felt so frustrated. There I was with what I thought was my terrible problem, and you seemed to be making a mountain out of a molehill."

"Well, you're right," Charlie started. "The horse did die, and it gets worse, it was all my fault."

"But how can it have been your fault–" Izzy looked shocked. "You have to tell me exactly what happened."

Charlie sat down on an upturned bucket, and put his head in his hands. "I suppose you might as well know the whole story," he went on, his hands shaking. "It was out on the training fields. We were galloping... the horse dropped away beneath me... she just dropped down dead. I was riding too fast..."

"Rubbish," Izzy said straightaway, in a self-assured voice. "There must be something more to it. You can't kill a horse by riding it. There must have been something wrong with her."

"I don't know." Charlie was unconvinced, in spite of Izzy's efforts to reassure him. Slowly, he rubbed his forehead. "I just don't know. The head lad at Elmwood seemed to think it was my fault... and Tom."

"Tom? You mean he knows about this?" Izzy looked surprised.

"Yes, I told him two days ago," Charlie said gloomily. "Tom was really shocked."

"But how can it have been your fault?" Izzy cried in exasperation. "Have you been back to the racing stables?"

"Well no," Charlie answered.

"Then why don't you go back and get some answers?" she asked, excitedly.

"I've tried that. I couldn't face going in." Charlie blurted the words out, the passion clear in his voice. "I don't want to go back there, and now I'm worried that Tom is going to tell Nick and Sarah."

"Hmm..." Izzy had an idea forming in her head.

"What is it?" Charlie asked, seeing the expression on Izzy's face.

"Well," she started slowly, "if you're riding again, Nick and Sarah don't ever need to know the truth about the accident, do they? They won't need to know that the horse actually died. Come on, Charlie," Izzy cried. "Why not try tomorrow when we're all at the Colcott Show? Why don't you take Napoleon out then – when there's no one to watch you?"

"Well." Charlie looked unconvinced by Izzy's plan. "Perhaps you're right," he said hesitantly. "Maybe I should have one last try. Maybe that would be the answer.

"Of course it is ," Izzy said enthusiastically, seeming to have forgotten her own problems. "Be determined.

Now, we need to talk more about this," she said,
leading him off to the tack room...

7

CATASTROPHE STRIKES

The morning of the Colcott Show dawned bright and clear. Since 6 o'clock, everyone had been rushing around madly, grooming, plaiting manes and oiling hooves. Charlie and Izzy had spent some time yesterday afternoon concocting a plan. They'd decided that Charlie would offer to stay behind and man the yard for Sarah. That way, she could go to the show, and Charlie would have the chance to take out Napoleon. And it had worked, the plan had all been agreed.

Now it was 8 o'clock and the yard was in chaos. Charlie was relieved to see that each of the horses and riders was nearly ready. It wouldn't be long now. He'd managed to avoid Tom all morning, hoping that if he kept out of the way, it wouldn't act as a prompt for Tom to tell Nick and Sarah.

"Hey Charlie. Have you told Nick and Sarah about the accident yet?" Tom hissed as they loaded the last of the horses into the horsebox.

"No," Charlie answered firmly, walking off.

"Well, you're running out of time – Nick's off on his training course tomorrow," Tom called from the cab of the horsebox. "Look, I'll catch you at the show. We'll talk about this later."

"I'm not coming to the show," Charlie answered.

"What? What do you mean you're not coming?" Tom said. "Don't you care enough to at least come and watch?"

Charlie shrugged his shoulders. "I'm staying behind to man the stables," he answered, his jaw jutting out defiantly.

"Well, please yourself, but if you're not going to tell Nick and give him a chance to help you ride, then maybe you should let go of your place at the British Racing School," Tom said crossly.

Charlie tried to look nonchalant, but he felt sick at Tom's throwaway lines. Give up his place at the British Racing School? Tom had hinted at it before, but he hadn't actually said it. The thought made Charlie feel terrible, and he was glad to see everyone pile into the Land Rover. They'd be gone soon.

"You will be all right won't you, Charlie?" Izzy whispered to him in passing.

"I'll be just fine," Charlie said, through gritted teeth.

"Well good luck then," she said. "Chin up. You can do it."

Charlie smiled weakly. "Good luck as well," he answered. Their conversation came to a close as Sarah summoned Izzy into the back of the Land Rover.

"Just take down a phone number with any bookings and say we'll confirm when we get back," Sarah called across to Charlie.

"OK," Charlie answered.

"It shouldn't be too busy. I think most people know we're at the show today," Sarah went on.

"Fine," Charlie replied.

At last everyone was ready. Doors were slammed shut and the horse box drove out of the yard. They were off.

"Bye." Charlie waved. But his words were drowned out by the sound of the engine. The last thing he saw was Izzy's face peering from the window as they drove out of the yard. Walking across to Napoleon's stable, Charlie thought about what Tom had said. More than anything he wanted to take up his place at the British Racing School. Charlie hated the way he felt, loathed the sick feeling in the pit of his stomach. Izzy was right. He had to do it. He had to get riding again.

As he crossed the yard, he stopped for a moment to fill up a haynet. He collected Napoleon's saddle and bridle and dumped them outside the stable, then he looked around him. Maybe he should tidy up a little. But, as Charlie turned and surveyed the yard, he knew that he was just prolonging the agony.

"Come on, you're being pathetic," he said to himself. Taking a deep breath, he approached Napoleon's stable.

"OK boy?" he said, looking inside. Napoleon ignored him.

"I'm sorry you're missing the show. It's all my fault, but I'm going to take you out for a ride now."

Somehow, saying things aloud helped Charlie get them off his chest and, if nothing else, he was starting to feel a little calmer.

Quickly he groomed Napoleon. Then, just as he was about to turn and pick up the bridle, he heard the sound of a Land Rover roll into the yard. Sarah was back! She must have forgotten something.

Charlie froze to the spot, not daring to look out over the box. He racked his brains to come up with something to say, the panic seizing hold of him. And then he heard a voice call out, and he breathed a sigh of relief. False alarm. It wasn't Sarah at all.

"Yoo hoo. Is anyone around?" A woman's voice echoed around the yard.

Charlie stepped forward and sneaked a look out of the corner of the box. A woman stood in the middle of the yard, a small girl by her side.

"Isn't this a lovely stables, Julia?" She turned to the small girl.

"Oh, it looks brilliant, Mummy," the girl answered.

"Now, where is everyone?" her mother started again, looking anxiously around her. "There must be someone here we can talk to."

Suddenly, Charlie felt very guilty that he had been planning to stay hidden as he stood inside the box. He'd heard the enthusiasm in their voices. He couldn't just leave them standing there. He took a deep breath, and backed out of the box.

"Can I help?" he asked.

"Oh good, there is someone about," the mother said, smiling. "We just wanted to book some lessons for Julia."

"Well, I'm afraid that the owners aren't here at the moment," Charlie answered. "They're at the Colcott Show today, but I can take a provisional booking and get them to confirm when they come back."

"That sounds fine," the mother answered. "So, tell me, is it as nice here as it looks?" she said brightly. "I used to be part of a similar sort of set-up when I was a girl, and I couldn't bear to go home at the end of each day," she laughed.

"Well, it's a great stables," Charlie started. "And Nick Brooks who runs it, is a brilliant instructor. He used to be a National Hunt jockey before he set up Sandy Lane."

"Really? And the standard of riding's good?" The mother looked interested.

"Yes... yes it is," Charlie said, feeling a complete fraud as the words spilled out. How could he enthuse about it all, when he wasn't even riding himself? He felt mean as he found himself wishing they would just go. They were doing a tour of the stables now. Shifting uneasily from one foot to the other, Charlie waited impatiently.

"Bye then. See you next Thursday," he called as they eventually got into their car again.

"Yes, bye," the little girl waved.

Charlie took a deep breath as they drove out of the yard, and quickly he walked across the gravel.

"We're still going out for that ride, Napoleon." He gritted his teeth determinedly. "You're not going to be let off the hook that easily." But Charlie sounded more confident than he felt.

"It's OK. It'll be OK," he said to himself.

The calm that Charlie had felt earlier had completely evaporated. As he reached up to put on the bridle, his fingers were all thumbs. He knew that he was being clumsy as he did up the throat lash. Now for the saddle.

Napoleon looked disgruntled as Charlie put the saddle down on his back. It was as though the horse could sense Charlie's unease. Charlie grimaced, hoping his reluctance to ride wasn't too obvious – animals were able to smell fear on humans.

"Come on boy... settle down," he said as Napoleon sidestepped around the stable.

Swiftly, Charlie led Napoleon out of his loose box and through the gate at the back of the yard. He was determined to take Napoleon as far away from the stables as was possible so there would be little chance of anyone surprising them. But the further Charlie walked, the harder it became to find a suitable place to stop and mount. The trees rustled in the breeze.

Charlie fixed his gaze into the distance. They were nearly at the furrowed fields now, and Napoleon was jogging by Charlie's side, getting more and more restless, until he was jumping at imaginary creatures in the hedgerow.

"Settle down," Charlie cried as Napoleon started to break into a raking trot, and Charlie found himself being pulled along. Quickly he managed to calm the horse back down to a walk. "We'll just go to the other end of this field, and then I'll get on," he said soothingly.

Charlie's stomach was tying itself in knots. His arms felt as though they were being yanked out of their sockets. Napoleon was sweating up with excitement, his eyes rolling as he jumped skittishly from side to side. Perhaps this wasn't a good idea after all. And then a low-flying military jet shot across the sky. Jets were commonplace around Colcott, but this one was followed by another and another. Napoleon flung his head high into the air, jerking the reins out of Charlie's hands.

Before Charlie knew it, the horse was off, swerving this way and that, galloping madly across the fields, as if his life depended on it.

"Napoleon, Napoleon," Charlie called, desperately chasing after him. Surely he'd slow down in a moment. But Napoleon wasn't stopping for anyone and, as the horse soared over the fence and galloped off in the direction of Larkfield Copse, Charlie realized with a sinking heart that he'd never catch him. Slowly, Charlie drew to a halt and bent over, desperately trying to get his breath back. He didn't know what to do. There wasn't anyone back at the yard to help him look for Napoleon either. One thing was for sure – he had to find that horse before everyone got back from the show. Nick would never forgive him if Napoleon came to any harm, and then that really would be the end of things for him at Sandy Lane.

8

CONFESSIONS

Without a horse to ride, it was a long walk back to the yard for Charlie. He collected his mountain bike, and then spent the next two hours cycling through field after field. He even combed Larkfield Copse, but no luck there. It was hot and muggy and Charlie felt irritable.

Desperately trying to think clearly, he made his way back to the stables. What should he do? He couldn't leave the yard unmanned any longer. He'd have to ring the police and report Napoleon missing and that meant facing up to the fact that the horse was truly lost.

Slowly, Charlie made his way into the tack room, dragging his feet as he flicked open the appointments book to get to the telephone section at the back. The number of the local police station was clearly written there in Nick's hand.

Charlie gripped the receiver tightly as he dialled the number and listened to what the police officer had to say. It seemed that all he could do was sit and wait. So that was exactly what Charlie did. He spent the rest of the afternoon sitting in the tack room, just willing the phone to ring.

And now it was 5 o'clock. Nick and the others were still at Colcott, oblivious to what he'd done. They'd be back soon. Time was running out.

Charlie didn't know what to think. He half wanted them to get back so he had someone to share the burden of it all, and yet the thought of telling Nick what had happened filled him with horror. Charlie sat staring into space.

Rrrring... rrrring. Charlie almost jumped out of his skin as the sound of the telephone echoed around the tack room and he lunged across the desk to grab the receiver.

"Yes, yes this is Sandy Lane," he answered, breathlessly. "Oh right." His heart sank. It was only someone calling to book a lesson. "Yes, no, I'm sorry... I mean, I thought you were going to be someone else. Yes, the 10 o'clock hack on Saturday's fine," he said, taking the details and putting down the phone.

Charlie looked at his watch. He was feeling desperate now. And then his heart skipped a beat as he heard a familiar engine in the distance. He felt sick as he looked out of the tack room window to see the horsebox roll into the yard. The others were back.

Silently he watched as his friends poured out of the various vehicles, laughing and shouting. The yard was immediately alight with activity. Ramps were lowered, rosette-laden horses were unloaded, and each of the riders set about their tasks. Slowly, Charlie got down from the stool and left the tack room, almost colliding with Tom on the way.

"Watch where you're going," Tom said, good-naturedly. "Hey, aren't you going to ask how Chancey and I did?"

But Charlie was already running across the yard, dodging this way and that through the various horses and riders. Tom's voice faded as Charlie headed into the cottage. He had to get to Nick before anyone noticed that Napoleon was missing. He poked his head around the kitchen door.

"Nick, Nick," he called, urgently.

"Yes, I'm just coming." Nick's voice answered him, and then he appeared.

"How did things go here?" he asked. "All right?" And then he noted Charlie's red face. "There isn't a problem is there?"

Charlie took a deep breath. "Well, actually there is, I'm afraid, um, it's Napoleon – you see, he's not in his stable any more."

"What do you mean he's not in his stable?" Nick looked puzzled. "Have you checked the fields at the back? Has someone put him out to graze? I'm sure I saw him earlier. Sarah... Sarah, have you seen

Napoleon?" he called.

"No Nick... I mean... I'm not explaining things clearly," Charlie started again. "I've accidentally let him go."

"You've let him go!" Nick looked startled. "When? Where?"

"Well, about three hours ago."

"Three hours ago!" Nick bellowed. "You mean to tell me he's been missing for three hours! What were you doing?"

"Well, I took him out for a ride, only I didn't get on straight away, and then there were some jets. They startled him. He tugged the reins right out of my hands and then he shot off."

"I haven't got time to listen to this now," Nick said. "We've got to find him. If he gets out onto the road there could be a serious accident, anything could happen. How could you have been so STUPID?"

Charlie stood rooted to the spot. He didn't know what to say.

"What's this?" Sarah had heard the shouting, and now she appeared in the doorway.

"Napoleon's gone," Nick said breathlessly.

"Gone?"

"Yes gone – escaped. He bolted with Charlie. We've got to let the police know."

"I've already done that," Charlie said, sounding calmer than he felt.

"Well, I'll just have to go and look for him myself then. Where was he heading?"

"Larkfield Copse," Charlie answered.

"I'll take the Land Rover over there," Nick said quickly.

"Shall I come with you?" Charlie asked.

"No." Nick looked furious. "You just stay here in case anyone phones." He grabbed his car keys and ran out of the back door.

The kitchen door slammed shut before Charlie had a chance to say anything more. He turned round to see Sarah standing behind him.

"I'm sorry," he said.

Sarah looked at him sympathetically. "I know Nick sounds harsh, but you've got to understand where he's coming from. You should never have taken a horse out on your own – you could have been hurt. We are responsible for you while your mother's away, you know. And what about Napoleon? Until he's back in one piece, none of us will be able to rest."

"I know, I know," Charlie answered. "I know that what I did was silly. I only thought that... if... well–"

What could he say? As far as Sarah was concerned, he'd been riding for the last week anyway. How could he tell her that it wasn't true? Charlie was wandering around the room now, restlessly dragging his hands through his hair.

"Charlie, just sit down," Sarah said. "You're making me feel nervous."

"I'm so sorry. I think I'd better go outside and get some air."

"That might be a good idea," Sarah said, calmly.

Charlie stepped out of the door and, as he looked up from the ground, a sea of faces rose to greet him. It was the last thing he needed. Suddenly, he was bombarded by question after question from all sides as his friends stood, waiting for explanations as to what was going on.

"What's happened?" Rosie asked.

"Nick looked furious," Jess added.

"Are you all right?" Tom looked concerned.

Charlie took a deep breath. "It's Napoleon... he bolted with me," he started. "I took him out for a ride, only I couldn't hold him," he said, embarrassed.

"You took Napoleon out for a ride?" Tom said.

"Yes." Charlie didn't know what to say as he looked at his friends. Izzy stood back from the crowd, looking decidedly sheepish. She was the only one who didn't say a word. Shamefaced, Charlie turned away and walked off to the tack room, the unanswered questions ringing in his ears.

9

AN UNEXPECTED GUEST

It was several hours before Nick arrived back at the yard – several hours that Charlie spent anxiously waiting in his room. The long summer day had drawn to a close and his friends had gone home. The dusk cast an eerie light over the stables. It should have been a happy end to a successful day for Sandy Lane. Tom had won the Open Jumping as expected, and the others had brought back a collection of rosettes from the gymkhana. But no one was really able to enjoy it.

Charlie jumped to his feet the moment the Land Rover arrived back and rushed down the stairs to the kitchen, but when Nick appeared at the door of the cottage, Charlie could tell by his expression that he hadn't found Napoleon. Helplessly Charlie stood, shuffling his feet about, not knowing what to say.

"Any calls?" Nick asked on entering the kitchen.

"Not a thing," Sarah answered. "I've rung the police every hour, on the hour. They're sick of the sound of me."

"And I've looked about everywhere I can imagine," Nick added. "So all we can do now is wait for news. I'm going to have a shower." He squeezed behind the kitchen chairs and made his way to the stairs.

"I'm sorry I yelled at you," he said, looking back at Charlie's pinched face. "It's just that I'm worried."

"I know, and I'm sorry for what I've done," Charlie answered. Nick's kind words were making him feel even worse and he felt a lump rising in his throat. "I didn't know what else to do, you see–"

"Not now, Charlie," Nick said, gently. "We'll talk about it later."

Charlie nodded and sat down. "Is there anything I can do to help, Sarah?" he offered.

"Well you could lay the table for supper," Sarah said. "Even if there has been a calamity, we still have to eat, and maybe it'll take our mind off things."

Charlie nodded and got up from the table to reach for the cutlery. In a daze, he counted out the knives and forks against the background hum of the television. Slowly, he made his way over to the window sill to get the table mats. It was dark outside and he couldn't see anything very clearly in the yard, but something stopped him. Was that a noise? He paused, mats in hand. No, his mind was just playing tricks on him. He was jumping at everything.

But there it was again, and louder now. This time Charlie was sure there was something outside.

He pressed his face against the window, staring out into the gloom of the night, and then he had the fright of his life. For there, on the other side of the window, a familiar face peered in at him. Charlie's heart skipped a beat. It was Napoleon! Napoleon was standing in Nick and Sarah's garden. Charlie gulped. If he was quiet, he might be able to creep around the back and catch him.

"What is it, Charlie?" Sarah said, looking up from the pan she was stirring. "You look as though you've seen a ghost."

"Sshh." Charlie motioned to his lips and pointed to the window. Shuffling slowly across the stone kitchen floor, he headed for the door. "Have you got a carrot?" he whispered.

Sarah nodded at the vegetable rack, and quickly Charlie grabbed a large carrot. He slipped out of the back door, and around the side of the house.

The bay horse stood perfectly still, munching contentedly at the grass. He had lost his saddle, and his reins trailed, muddy and broken, by his side, but he appeared to be in one piece.

Charlie walked slowly and lightly so as not to disturb him.

At that moment Napoleon seemed to sense Charlie's presence. He lifted his head, his ears twitching inquisitively.

"Come on boy," Charlie said softly. "Nice carrot

here for you."

Napoleon looked wary as Charlie leaned forward, but still he didn't move. Charlie hardly dared breathe. And then, with a swish of his tail, Napoleon stumbled over and gratefully accepted the offering. Before he even had a chance to move away, Charlie had grabbed the reins.

"You bad, bad boy," Charlie said in a gentle voice, relief flooding through him now that the horse was safely caught. "Where have you been all day? What have you been up to? We've been worried sick. You had me in serious trouble." Charlie turned round to find Sarah standing behind him.

"Thank goodness," she said. "He's back."

There was a sound of feet pounding down the stairs and suddenly Nick appeared at Sarah's shoulder. A grin spread across his face.

"I don't believe it," he said.

"I don't know what he can have been up to, but he's absolutely caked in mud," Sarah laughed.

Charlie turned around and looked properly at the horse now. It was true. His coat was matted in whorls where he must have been rolling, and briars and twigs were twisted in his mane. Still, at least he was back in one piece.

"I'll take him back to his stable and groom him," Charlie offered. "I know I've got a lot of explaining to do," he mumbled, without looking directly at Nick.

"We can talk about all that over supper," Nick said seriously as Charlie led the horse off.

Charlie nodded. The thought of sitting down and actually going through the whole story with Nick and Sarah filled him with dread. But he'd have to do it. They'd been so patient with him. He owed it to them. He'd have to tell them the truth... about everything.

10

THE TRUTH OF THE MATTER

"That's quite a story, Charlie," Nick said calmly. "It explains a lot – why you wouldn't ride, the way you've been acting. Losing a horse is a very traumatic experience, and one I can completely relate to. If only you'd told us, I wouldn't have put so much pressure on you."

"I just didn't know what you'd say." Charlie looked despondent. "I thought you'd blame me. I can't believe you're being so good about it. You see I told Tom, and he was shocked."

"Tom? Well it's probably a bit harder for someone to understand when they haven't actually been through it all before."

Charlie looked up expectantly. Sarah stood up at

that moment. "I'm beat, I think I'll go to bed. I'm glad it's all out in the open, Charlie," she said. "Goodnight."

As the door closed on Sarah, Nick started again. "You see, something like this happened to me," he said. "A horse of mine, Golden Fleece, died in an accident too, so I sort of know what you're going through."

"Golden Fleece DIED?" Charlie was shocked. He'd heard so much about the amazing racehorse from Nick's National Hunt days, but he didn't realize she'd been killed in an accident.

"Yes, she died," Nick said sadly. "I don't like talking about it much. I stopped racing soon after it happened. I remember thinking at the time that I would never even ride again. But I was wrong about that, it just took time."

Charlie opened his mouth to speak, and then closed it again, judging it best to keep quiet and let Nick tell the story in his own way. "Well, you've never really told any of us what happened, Nick."

"It upsets me," Nick began. "Even now I don't like talking about Golden Fleece." He took a deep breath. "It happened a while ago, but it's still clear in my mind. It was a long time before I could truly put it behind me," he sighed. "It's the real reason I gave up racing altogether and set up Sandy Lane. You see, when Golden Fleece fell and broke her leg, I thought I was somehow responsible, and I couldn't forgive myself for that. It took me some time to realize that it wasn't my fault. Who could have predicted that the leading horse would fall in front of Golden Fleece and bring her down? Who could have predicted that she would land so awkwardly? And me – well I wasn't even hurt – not seriously."

Charlie looked embarrassed, seeing the pain in Nick's face.

"But accidents do happen, Charlie," Nick went on. "In all walks of life. Racing, like any other sport, has its fair share of them, but they're one-offs – chance happenings that we should learn to accept rather than dwell on too deeply."

Nick stared into the distance. "I've made another life for myself now, but you – you've got your whole racing career ahead of you. Don't throw it away." He stopped abruptly. "Look, I'm afraid I'm going to have to get on with my reading tonight if I'm going to be up to date for this course tomorrow, but when I come back from the course, I'll phone Josh and find out what really happened. Try not to worry. Horses don't just die for no reason at all. We'll sort out a training programme for you. Try not to think about this O'Grady. I'm sure he was just upset. I'll get you riding again, you'll see," he said.

"Well, I don't know," Charlie said, tentatively. Nick frowned.

"No honestly. It's just that I've tried everything to get riding again, and I just don't think I can do it," Charlie went on.

"Yes you can," Nick said firmly.

68

Charlie smiled, but didn't say anything more as he got to his feet. He felt a whole lot better now that everything was out in the open and, as he cleared the table, he realized how grateful he was that Nick had been willing to listen.

"I'll do the washing up," Charlie offered.

"Thanks," Nick said as he made his way into the adjoining sitting room with his book.

Charlie wiped the last plate dry and looked at Nick in the chair. It had been a long day and he seemed tired. Charlie felt bad as he watched him trying to keep his eyes open to read.

"I'm going to bed now," Charlie called to Nick.

"OK," he answered. "Oh Charlie," he called him back. "Make sure you look after Sarah for me while I'm away, won't you? You know what she's like – she'll start grooming or mucking out before you know it, and with the baby due in three weeks it's important she doesn't take on too much. I wouldn't put it past her to try getting on a horse!"

"I'll do my best," Charlie answered.

"And don't be afraid to phone me if you need to," Nick went on. "Although I'll be telephoning Sandy Lane regularly to keep a check on things anyway."

"OK," Charlie answered, knowing full well that it would take a real emergency before he'd bother him at the course. Nick had been waiting ages to get a place. Charlie didn't want to trouble Nick with anything that might mess it up.

"Well goodnight then," Nick said. "Do you think

you could try to be up early so we can go through rotas and things before I leave?"

"Yes of course," Charlie said, anxious to do anything to help. "Goodnight Nick," he answered, closing the door and heading up the stairs to his bedroom.

It was a muggy night, oppressively hot and still, and Charlie's head felt fuzzy as he walked over to the desk in his room and pulled open the top drawer. Settling down onto the bed, he curled his feet back under him. Slowly, he leafed through the brochure he had taken out, flicking through page after page of glossy pictures.

It was the British Racing School prospectus, now rather well-thumbed and worn. But for Charlie, it held a glimpse of what his future might hold. He hadn't looked at it for three weeks now... three whole weeks. Suddenly he had a flashback to Tom's words before the Colcott Show.

'If you're not going to ride, you ought to give up your place at racing school... give someone else a chance of getting in.' Tom had said it in anger, but it had stuck in Charlie's mind.

He paused for a moment as he leafed through the prospectus and stared at the phone number on the back. Could he believe Nick when he'd said he'd get him riding again? Or should he call the school in the morning and withdraw?

Slowly, Charlie got up from his bed and walked back across the room. He wouldn't do it just yet.

He'd trust Nick on this one. Quickly he stuffed the prospectus firmly back in the drawer it had come from and turned the key.

11

STORM BREWING

When Charlie woke the next morning, it was to a very different day from the one before. It was grey... thunderously grey and dark, and the sky had a murky green tinge to it. Charlie was tired after all the emotion of last night, and longed to roll back into sleep, but he knew he had to get up. Nick was off today, and had specifically asked him to be up early to help.

Charlie heaved himself out of bed and crossed the room to open his bedroom windows. A heavy smell of rain hung in the air. He pulled on his clothes and hurried down the stairs to where Nick and Sarah were sitting at the kitchen table.

"Morning," Nick said. "Are you ready to go over everything?"

"Sure Nick," Charlie answered.

"Well, I've cancelled all the lessons while I'm away, so there are only hacks going out." Nick got straight to the point. "And Tom's agreed to take care of those. Of course Sarah will be around all the time, but if you could bring the horses in from the fields as usual, and give them their morning feeds, that would be great."

"All right, Nick," Charlie said, grateful that even though he wasn't riding, Nick was still giving him tasks to fill his time.

"You'll need to make sure the horses are fed at lunchtime too," Nick started, talking through a mouthful of cereal. "But don't let any of them go out for at least an hour afterwards, OK?"

"OK."

"Good," Nick grinned. "Well, I'm going to be off in about half an hour, so let's go and get the horses in."

"OK," Charlie answered.

"I'll leave the phone number of where I'm staying on the pin board."

"That's fine," Charlie answered and, as Nick got up from the table, he followed him out into the yard.

It was quiet outside as Charlie grabbed a bunch of head collars and followed Nick into the fields at the back.

Quickly, all of the horses were caught and put in their stables. As Charlie led Storm Cloud across the yard, he looked up to see Izzy cycling up the drive.

Quickly, she skidded to a halt. She looked expectantly at Charlie.

"Well?" she said, as she propped her bike up on the water trough.

"Well what?" Charlie looked puzzled.

"Well – is Napoleon back?"

With everything else that had happened last night, and all the rushing around that morning, Napoleon's disappearance had clean flown out of Charlie's mind.

"Yes, he's back," Charlie grinned.

"Phew, thank goodness." Izzy looked relieved. "You don't know how guilty I felt when I heard what had happened."

"It wasn't your fault," Charlie said fairly. "How were you to know I'd bodge everything."

"Oh, you didn't–" Izzy started, embarrassed. And so she changed the subject. "I couldn't even call you last night either – not with Nick and Sarah hanging around. I wanted to be here early to talk to you. What happened?"

"I'll tell you later, Izzy," Charlie said. "I didn't ride, but I'm more determined than ever now, and Nick's going to sort out a training programme for me when I get back. It's just that I can't bear to go through the whole story again."

"Oh." Izzy looked a bit put out, but knew when to keep quiet. And then Tom appeared, cycling into the yard. Charlie watched as Tom walked over to Nick and they stood, flicking through the appointments book.

"Charlie," Nick called across.

Reluctantly, Charlie ambled over to them. Things just hadn't been the same between him and Tom lately.

Tom didn't say a word at his approach, just stood there, hands deep in pockets. Charlie shifted his weight from one foot to the other as Nick started doling out the rest of the instructions.

"That's the lot then," Nick said. "Do you think you can manage it between you?"

"I should think so," Tom said confidently.

"Yes that's fine," Charlie added.

"Good, well if you want to go into the tack room, you can decide how you're going to divide up the chores," Nick said firmly, looking from one boy to the other.

The two of them nodded as Nick held out the book.

"I'm just going to nip back into the house to say goodbye to Sarah, and then I'll be off."

"OK," they said in unison.

Neither of the boys said anything to the other and Charlie hurried off to Napoleon's stable. Five minutes later, Nick appeared at the cottage, holdall in hand.

"Bye everyone," he called, striding over to the Land Rover. "See you Wednesday. And remember – call if you need me," he added.

"OK Nick," everyone answered.

"Well, I'd better get a move on if I'm going to get Chancey ready for the 9 o'clock hack," Tom said, quickly turning away.

Charlie made his way to Napoleon's stable.

"Hi, Charlie," Rosie called across the yard. "I hear Napoleon's been found. That's great news."

"Yes, Nick told us you did well to catch him," Alex added.

Charlie felt pleased that all of the gang were together, and for the first time in ages he felt more a part of it. "Well he found us really," he said modestly. "I think he knew that the best grass in the area was in Nick and Sarah's garden."

"Well, at least he's back safe and sound," Alex said, good-naturedly. "And I don't know about you, but Tom's given me my jobs for the day – four loose boxes to muck out, five haynets to fill, two horses to groom... that should keep me going for a while," he grinned. "How am I ever going to find the time to ride?"

Charlie laughed at Alex's mock-serious face. Awkwardly, he turned to Tom.

"Where shall we start then?" he asked.

****

The morning passed quietly and Charlie was relieved to find that things ran smoothly in Nick's absence. Sarah popped her head around the tack room door from time to time, but mostly she left them to it. It wasn't until 5 o'clock that any of the regular riders had time to go out for a hack, and by then it was bucketing down with rain.

"Typical," Rosie grimaced, looking out of the tack room window.

"It's only a summer shower," Charlie said.

"It's all right for you to say," Rosie moaned. "You're not riding."

The sentence slipped out so naturally, and Charlie knew Rosie didn't mean it unkindly, but still he couldn't stop himself from visibly wincing.

"Oh I didn't mean it like that, Charlie," Rosie started. "I just–"

"Don't worry," Charlie said, cutting her off midsentence. "I've got to tack up Storm Cloud for her rider anyway," he said, swiftly leaving the tack room.

But as he hurried across the yard, raincoat held protectively over his head, he thought about what Rosie had said. Well, it wouldn't be long before Nick was back and then he'd be riding again, wouldn't he?

Quickly, he tacked up Storm Cloud, his mind straying as he led the fragile Arab mare out of her stable. Patiently, he held her head for the rider to mount, and then he stood and watched as the riders clattered off down the drive.

"Bye," Charlie called, ducking into the tack room and out of the rain.

The sky looked thundery and forbidding and drops of water trickled down his back as he settled down to clean the tack. Not ideal weather to be riding, he thought, trying to convince himself that he wouldn't have wanted to be out on a day like this anyway.

The time passed quicker than Charlie had expected, and before he knew it six riders, soaked through to the skin, arrived back in the yard.

"It was awful, Charlie," Rosie called into the tack room. "We tried to ride to the lighthouse, but it was so windy we had to give up halfway. I'm drenched through. Can you help us with the horses?"

"Sure," Charlie answered, looking at the rain teeming down outside.

Normally he would have hated the idea of getting wet, but he was eager to join in and help out and, with a lighter heart, he stepped outside. For the next half hour, he ran around the yard, helping the others get the horses stabled and bedded for the night.

The rain was pelting down, and Charlie was so wet that by the end of it, his hair lay plastered to his head in tendrils.

At last the stable doors were shut and bolted. It had been a long day and Charlie felt pleased to be calling out his goodbyes to his friends.

"See you tomorrow," he shouted across the yard,

racing into the cottage and out of the rain.

"Oh Charlie, look what you're doing." Sarah's voice greeted him as he splashed puddles across the kitchen floor.

"Sorry Sarah," Charlie sneezed.

"I think you'd better go and have a hot bath straight away," she said.

"Thanks," Charlie said, gratefully.

Quickly, he made his way to his bedroom. Shutting the door behind him, Charlie peeled off his wet clothes and grabbed a towel to wrap around him. Crossing the landing, he hurried to the bathroom.

Charlie felt shivery as he turned the bath taps on full blast. Soon the steam filled the little room and almost immediately he started to feel better. The hot water nearly scalded his feet as he stepped into the bath. Lying back, he let the heat seep through his bones. The bathroom was at the top of the cottage, high in the attic, and the rain pelted hard on the roof top above his head. Charlie felt comforted that he was inside in the warm.

A clap of thunder rang out, and Charlie's face was aglow as lightning streaked across the sky. He closed his eyes and let himself relax into thought. Slowly, he let the images of the accident flood his mind. He replayed it... all of it, following it through from start to finish, and this time he didn't allow the panic to take hold of him. The gallops, the horse falling, the aftermath – all of the pictures flashed through his mind, and yet he didn't feel that monumental panic.

Taking a deep breath, Charlie immersed his head under the water, letting the warmth flood over him and drown out the noise of the gale.

12

STORMY AFTERMATH

Charlie slept better that night... completely slept through the noise of the storm that blew up outside. The window panes rattled heavily in their frames and the rain pelted rhythmically against the glass like tiny hammer blows, but Charlie was lulled into a deeper slumber than he'd had for some time.

When he woke the next day, the storm had blown over, but he was completely unprepared for the devastation it had wreaked. Sticks and branches lay strewn around the yard, and worse still, one of the fir trees lining the paddock had crashed through the end stable. Luckily, the box was empty, so none of the horses had been hurt, but all the same, it wasn't good news. The sky was clear and a cool breeze flitted around the stable yard.

"OK, now I don't mean to be bossy, but we've got a lot of work to do in the yard this morning." Sarah looked worried as the regulars gathered around to hear what she had to say. Charlie looked at the equally anxious faces of his friends as they stood waiting for instructions.

"I'll do as much as I can to clear things up," she went on. "But if you could go around collecting all the debris, that would be a great help."

"Have you told Nick about this, Sarah?" Tom started.

"No, the phone lines are down, so I haven't been able to speak to him. It's probably a good thing he doesn't know. He'd only worry, and he needs to be concentrating on the course. Anyway, do you think you could all make a start on things?" She suddenly sounded weary as she headed back to the cottage.

"Are you OK, Sarah?" Charlie said, following her into the kitchen. "You look as though you've seen a ghost."

"I'm fine," Sarah breathed softly. "It's just that – oh, it's all such a mess this happening while Nick's away. I wasn't going to say anything to you lot, but I can't find the insurance documents for the yard. I remember Nick saying ages ago that he was going to look out a cheaper policy. I don't know if he ever renewed the old one... argh, I'll kill him if he hasn't got it sorted. I can't phone the insurance company while the lines are down. I can't do anything," she said in despair. "Look, I think I'm going to have to go into Colcott and phone Nick from there. Could you keep charge of the yard for me while I'm gone?"

"Sure," Charlie said, glad to help in any way.

"Thank you," Sarah said appreciatively. "That would be great. I'll just get my coat." She disappeared up the stairs as Charlie slipped out into the yard.

Charlie was pleased to see everyone going about their tasks with gusto, and the debris of the storm was stacked in a pile over by the barn quicker than he'd imagined possible. As Charlie bent down to pick up a couple of branches, he smiled to himself. It was so like everyone at Sandy Lane to pitch in and help out. And then Tom passed by. Charlie turned away.

"How about you come over to my house for supper tonight, Charlie?" Tom offered. "We could go to the cinema."

"That would be great," Charlie smiled, wishing he'd thought of it first. "Let's go and get the horses ready for the 10 o'clock," he went on, turning back to Napoleon's stable.

"OK," Tom answered.

Ten minutes later, the horses were tacked up and Tom was leading the ride out of the yard.

"I'll see you later to sort out arrangements for this evening, Charlie," he said, twisting around in the saddle from Chancey's back.

The horses settled into their easy strides and walked down the drive just as Sarah arrived back in the Land Rover.

"Well, at least that's one thing sorted out," she called, looking a lot happier than when she had left. "The insurance is in place," she went on, jumping out of the Land Rover. "And the phone people are coming this afternoon."

"Did you get through to Nick?" Charlie asked.

"Yes, I've let him know the lines are down, so at least he won't worry if he can't get through. I haven't told him about this little catastrophe though," she said, pointing at the end stable. The insurance people are sending a claim form." Sarah gave a sigh. "Now, I'm absolutely exhausted after all that. I might go and put my feet up."

"Is there anything I can do to help?" Charlie asked.

"If you could just carry on running the yard, I'd be grateful." Sarah smiled at him.

"Of course, that's fine," Charlie answered, as she hurried back into the cottage. And then she poked her head out of the door again.

"Charlie," she called him back.

"Yes," he looked up.

"Thanks."

"That's OK." Charlie felt a warm glow flood through him, pleased that for once he was doing something right.

13

SARAH PANICS

"I can't believe they still haven't turned up." It was 6 o'clock that evening, and Sarah was pacing up and down the hallway, anxiously picking up the phone and putting it back down again, as if by so doing she might miraculously get it working. The line remained dead though, and Charlie didn't know what he could say to calm her.

"Even if I go into town and call, I bet the telephone people won't be there now," Sarah said crossly. "And I'd probably only get caught in another downpour anyway. I don't know what this weather's playing at."

The grey sky shrouded the cottage in a dull, empty light, adding a sense of gloom to the evening. "I'll give them until tomorrow, and then I really will start getting annoyed," she added.

Sarah already looked pretty annoyed to Charlie. It was a nuisance that the phone lines were down, and no doubt Sarah really wanted to talk to Nick, but there was nothing he could do about it.

"Do you think you might have missed them while you were resting?" Charlie asked.

"Even if I did, it shouldn't stop them from fixing the outside lines, should it?" Sarah said, crossly.

"No, no I suppose not," Charlie said, quietly.

His remark hadn't gone down that well, and he judged it might be best to keep out of Sarah's way. He turned for the stairs and paused.

"I'm going out soon, Sarah," he called. "Tom's invited me to his house for supper, and then we're going to the cinema. I could always try and call the telephone people from Tom's."

"Oh no, don't bother," Sarah said. "We'll leave it till tomorrow. I'm sorry, Charlie," she said. "I don't know quite what's come over me. I didn't mean to take it out on you."

"That's all right," Charlie answered, hanging around in the doorway. "Look, if you'd rather I didn't go out then—"

"No, you must go, Charlie," Sarah said, firmly. "Will you be all right getting to Tom's house, or do you want a lift?"

"No, I'll be fine. I'm going there on my bike, but thanks all the same. Tom's mum said she'll drive us to the cinema, and drop me back here afterwards."

"OK," said Sarah. "So what time should I expect

you back then?"

"About eleven," Charlie said, quickly.

"Fine," Sarah said. "But no later than that, OK? I don't want to sound like an old battleaxe, but whilst your mother's away, I am responsible for you." She smiled.

"OK," Charlie answered. Hopefully she'd be in bed when he got back, and no doubt she'd be back to her usual self by tomorrow. Hurrying into the hall, Charlie grabbed his jacket from the coat rack.

"Good night," he called out.

"Good night," Sarah answered.

Charlie headed for the door. Sprinting across the yard, he grabbed his bike and set off for Tom's house.

****

Sarah didn't know what to do with herself now that Charlie had gone. The cottage was very quiet. She walked over to the window and drew the curtains. Then she crossed over to the sink and turned the taps on full burst, letting the basin fill up with soapy suds.

She was completely unprepared for the severe pain that gripped her stomach. Slowly, she turned back to the dishes, but the pain grew stronger. Sarah clutched at her stomach. It was like nothing she'd ever felt before. She'd had a pain in her back that morning, but the baby wasn't due for another two and a half weeks – surely it hadn't started already. She groaned and turned to the back door, bending slightly to relieve the pain. Tugging the handle, she pulled it wide.

"Charlie, Charlie," she groaned. "Are you still there?"

But Charlie had disappeared, and there was no reply from the depths of the yard. Sarah's heart sank. What should she do? The phones were still down, and she certainly couldn't drive. She tried to think. And then the pain came again, much fiercer this time. She tried to breathe deeply as she gripped the kitchen table, unable to move.

14

RIDE BY MOONLIGHT

Charlie walked up the drive to the stables, whistling happily to himself. He'd had a good evening with Tom. It had been awkward at first – neither of them knowing what to say, and the silences over supper had been uncomfortable. No one had said much on the way to the cinema either, but after the film they'd stopped for an ice cream, and then everything had come pouring out.

At first, Tom had looked serious as Charlie had described the panic he'd felt when Napoleon had torn the reins out of his hands. But as the situation eased, the pair of them had found themselves laughing and joking, even laying bets on whether Sarah's baby would be a boy or a girl. The evening had passed all too quickly, so that when Tom's mum dropped Charlie at the bottom of Sandy Lane, the two boys decided to meet up at nine the next morning.

Charlie looked at his watch now. It was half past eleven. He felt a little guilty as he remembered that he'd told Sarah he'd be back by eleven.

Charlie could just make out the shape of the cottage as he walked on up the drive, but all was dark and silent. Stumbling over the doorstep, he fumbled to find his keys and then, turning the lock, he pushed open the back door. Silently, he tiptoed through the kitchen and into the hallway, groping along the wall.

"Charlie, Charlie, is that you?" a weak voice called out.

Charlie's heart skipped a beat. Something was wrong. Immediately he switched on a light and burst into the sitting room. There, he found Sarah, crouched over the sofa. She looked as white as a sheet, and her forehead was bathed in sweat. Charlie stood rooted to the spot in fear.

"What's happened?" he cried, pulling himself together as he rushed to her side.

"I think the baby's coming," she grimaced. "It's too soon. I'm scared, Charlie. What if something's terribly wrong?" she said, breathing heavily. "I don't know what's happening to me. I've got to get help. Can you call for an ambulance?"

"Of course I can," Charlie said, running to grab the phone. "How long have you been like this?" he cried, the panic seizing hold of him as he keyed in the numbers. Frantically, he thwacked the button, trying to get a dialling tone.

"It's still not working," Sarah gasped. "You're going to have to go and get help."

"Don't panic," Charlie started. "Just stay where you are."

"Does it look like I'm going anywhere?" Sarah gasped, managing a joke through the pain.

"OK... OK... I'm off," Charlie said, and quickly he darted out of the back door.

The moon was high in the sky, and an eerie white light filtered across the yard, giving a sort of electric feel to the air. Charlie raced over to the barn to collect his bike, and then he remembered. No bike – it was at Tom's. What could he do? Frantically, he looked around the yard. The Land Rover was there, but he didn't know how to drive, and he was too young anyway. He'd just have to run for help. He'd have to sprint like mad – the nearest people lived in the cottages over by Bucknell Woods, and that was a good two miles away.

Charlie didn't hesitate. He didn't even stop to think. Madly, he tore down the driveway, his arms flailing out in the still night air. Quickly, he plunged around the corner of the drive, past the duck pond, and sprinted into Sandy Lane. A yellow glow from the cottages in the distance lighted his way and Charlie pushed himself faster and faster until he thought his lungs might burst.

On and on he raced, until his legs felt like jelly. He

knew he was going to have to stop. Unwittingly, he found his pace slackening off until he was going no faster than a crawl. And still the comforting cottage lights were a long way off. He'd never reach them in time. Charlie strained his eyes to stare into the distance, and felt the panic seizing hold of him.

He thought hard. What should he do? Maybe he should turn back to the yard and get help some other way, some quicker way. Yes, that was it. And so Charlie double-backed on himself, willing his legs to start all over again.

"Not far now," he muttered as he jogged back to the yard. "We'll soon be there."

Charlie turned back up the drive, not really having a fixed plan of action in his mind. He took a deep breath and looked over to Napoleon's stable, gnawing at his bottom lip. Cross-country was by far the quickest way to the nearest cottage. He trembled as Napoleon lifted his head over the stable door and whinnied loudly.

And then Charlie knew he couldn't stand there deliberating any longer. Sarah could be in danger... Sarah's baby could be in danger. He'd have to do it.

Not stopping to think any more about it, Charlie sped into the tack room and grabbed Napoleon's bridle. There wasn't time for a saddle. He hurried across the yard and fumbled his way into the dark of the stable.

"Easy Napoleon, easy does it," he crooned.

Putting the bit in the horse's mouth and throwing

the bridle on over his head, Charlie fastened the throat lash and led the horse out into the yard.

He gulped hard and clenched the muscles in his cheeks. Then he threw himself onto Napoleon and rode bareback into the silvery night.

"Go on," he cried, urging his horse on. Effortlessly, they galloped across the grass, heading for the scrubland ahead. Charlie bent his head low to shield himself from the coastal wind as they crossed the fields.

It wasn't until they approached the overhang of Bucknell Woods that Charlie slowed Napoleon down to a trot. It was dark ahead of them, and for the first time, Charlie realized how difficult it was going to be to see his way through the thicket. Here, where the tops of the trees masked the moonlit sky, he couldn't see a thing.

He squinted, tentatively nudging Napoleon on. Which way should they take to get to the road? All of the paths looked identical.

Charlie took a deep breath. The smell of pine clung in the air as he navigated a path through the trees, heading this way and that. Napoleon was sweating up, excited by the adventure, and he pulled at the reins. Surely they'd come this way only a minute ago. Charlie wasn't sure. He felt as though his arms were being yanked out of their sockets. They were lost in the deepest depths of a wood, and Charlie didn't know which way to turn.

The night was very still. Suddenly, Charlie felt

really scared as he listened for a sound in the distance... anything. And then they turned into a clearing and Charlie's heart soared as the moonlight streamed through the trees. That was the sound of a car in the distance. They must be nearing the road.

Charlie turned Napoleon down the path and nudged him on, almost sliding off his back as they broke into a trot. The beam from a car's headlights flashed through the woods, almost blinding him. Charlie raised his arm to shield his eyes from the glow. They were at the road. Nudging Napoleon on, they crossed the road, the horse's hooves echoing hollowly on the tarmac. Charlie's eyes were beginning to stream with water as the wind bit into his face and they rode faster and faster along the grass verge.

And slowly, surely, the cottages ahead of Charlie came into shape. They were shrouded in darkness, and whoever lived in them had obviously already gone to bed. Charlie stopped at the first one. He'd have to wake someone up.

Quickly, Charlie turned to the gate and jumped to the ground. Taking care to tie Napoleon to the fence, he hurried up the path to the front door and knocked loudly. No answer. Charlie started to panic. He ran around the side and pressed his nose to the window, but he couldn't see a thing. He ran back to the door and hammered his fists against it. For a moment, Charlie thought that no one was going to answer him. Then a dog started barking. That would wake someone up, surely?

"Can you hear me?" Charlie shouted, banging furiously on the door. "Please answer." And then a yellow light came on in the upstairs window.

"Hurry, hurry," he muttered under his breath. Charlie heard the rattle of a chain and a bolt was drawn back. The door opened just a fraction and an old lady looked out through the crack.

"I'm not here to hurt you," Charlie said quickly. "But could you phone for an ambulance for me? Please? It's an emergency. I've come from Sandy Lane. The owner's having a baby."

The old lady didn't do anything, seeming not to understand Charlie's words. A weighty silence hung in the air. "Please," he begged.

For a grim moment, Charlie thought that the woman was going to close the door on him... that his words were going to have no effect, but then something in his voice must have stirred her because the next thing he knew, the chain was sliding back from the door and she let him in.

"You can use the phone," she said, pointing to where it sat in the hallway.

"Thank you, oh thank you," Charlie breathed as he grabbed the receiver.

"999... ambulance please." He turned his attention to the voice at the other end.

"Yes, I need an ambulance at Sandy Lane Stables... yes, Mrs. Brooks, the owner, has gone into labour. Yes, Sandy Lane, off the Bucknell Road."

Charlie felt relieved as he put the phone down. They were on their way.

"I'm so sorry to have woken you," he said to the old lady. "The phones at the stables haven't been working all day and I've had to ride here." Charlie gabbled the words out.

"That's all right." The old lady seemed to have regained her composure and showed only concern now. "Would you like to sit down for a moment? Perhaps have a cup of tea?"

"No, no, that's quite all right, but thank you anyway." Charlie was already halfway down the path. "I've got to get back to the stables," he said as he stumbled over to Napoleon and gathered up the reins.

He led the horse over to a clear spot to mount. "I don't believe it – I rode here." Charlie rubbed his forehead with his hands in disbelief, and suddenly the enormity of the whole situation dawned on him. He had managed to ride... actually ride.

Quickly he sprang up onto Napoleon's back. He paused for a fraction of a second before urging Napoleon on towards Sandy Lane.

He didn't fancy finding his way through those dark woods again, so he rode Napoleon down the quiet, moonlit road. It was a longer route, but help was on its way. Charlie nudged Napoleon into a trot. If it weren't for the image of Sarah's white, panic-stricken face in his mind, he might even have felt a little thrill of exhilaration. He was riding again!

15

A LONG WAIT

Charlie pushed Napoleon on more quickly and they headed for the stables. The sound of the horse's hooves on the road rang out clearly into the still of the night.

Charlie felt numb as he adjusted his seat to the easy rise and fall of Napoleon's trot. Riding was the easy part now. Not knowing what would be waiting for him when he got back was beginning to prey on his mind. He hoped that Sarah would be all right. As he made the last turn down the lane, he could see a blue flashing light hanging over the yard. He took a deep breath. The ambulance must be there – at least Sarah would be in safe hands. Quickly, Charlie turned up the driveway.

He was greeted by a flurry of activity. For the first few moments no one seemed to notice him, but as he jumped down from Napoleon and led him into his box, one of the ambulance men called over.

"Are you the boy who phoned?"

"Yes, yes I am," Charlie said, breathlessly. "I live here, I mean, I'm staying with the Brooks' at the moment. Is Sarah going to be all right?"

"She'll be fine, but the baby's on its way," the man answered. "We've got to get her to the hospital fast. She's been asking for her husband."

"He's away on a training course at the moment," Charlie said. "I'll try and get hold of him and let him know what's happened."

"If you could," the man replied.

"The phones are down here," Charlie said. "Can I come with you?"

"Yes, but hurry," the ambulance man said. "We're going."

"I'll just get the number." Charlie dashed into the cottage, grabbed the note from beside the phone, and locked the back door of the cottage. The instant he was in the ambulance, it was being driven out of the yard. Charlie looked at Sarah's white face as he sat down, and she smiled.

The ambulance drove speedily along the winding back roads. The blue light was flashing away as they passed through the surrounding villages, until they reached the outskirts of Colcott.

"Not far now," one of the ambulance men said

reassuringly.

As they pulled up outside the hospital, the blue light was still flashing away. Charlie stood to one side as Sarah was lowered to the ground on her trolley.

"You'll be all right," he whispered.

"Thanks," Sarah said as they wheeled her away. "Could you try and get hold of Nick for me?" she asked.

"Sure I'll do that," Charlie said.

"Are you OK?" One of the nurses was walking over to him now. "You came in the ambulance, didn't you?"

"Yes," Charlie answered. "Yes I did."

"Well, Mrs. Brooks is going to the delivery room now. You can sit in the waiting room over there."

"OK," Charlie started. "I need to use the phone though."

But the nurse was off and out of earshot before he had a chance to explain that he needed to call Nick. Wearily, he took himself off in search of a phone. Heading down the nearest corridor, he came to a refreshments area. It was deserted, but there was a call box. Luckily he had the right coins in his pocket. He got out the piece of paper with Nick's number on it. He hoped that someone would be awake.

Impatiently, he shifted his weight from one foot to the other as he waited for a connection. The phone rang and rang. There *must* be someone there. They must answer eventually... surely. Then he heard a voice at the other end.

"Yes, hello, do you know what time this is?" It came loud and clear.

"I'm sorry. I need to talk to Nick Brooks," he said. "It's an emergency."

It was another few moments before Nick came to the phone.

"Nick–" Charlie started.

"Who's that? What's going on?"

"It's Charlie here... Sarah's gone into labour. We're at the hospital, but she's asking for you."

There was silence from the other end, and Charlie began again. "I didn't know what to do," he babbled. "I didn't know where to go – you see the phones were down at Sandy Lane, and I couldn't get help any other way. I'd left my bike at Tom's, so I had to ride... I had to ride–"

"Look, I'll be right with you. You're at Colcott Hospital, are you?" Nick said. "It's going to take me a few hours to get there. I'll leave right now."

That wrapped up the conversation. Charlie put down the hand set, and wearily found his way back to the room the nurse had pointed out. Quietly he settled down in a chair to wait for news, and suddenly he realized how tired he was. He was exhausted, both mentally and physically. His eyes felt heavy with sleep. Charlie let out a loud yawn. Try as he might, he couldn't stay awake, and finally he allowed himself to succumb to tiredness. In no time at all, he had drifted off into sleep. In his dreams though, he was cantering through the fields on Napoleon's back... this time not as if Sarah's life depended on it, but for enjoyment – for pure pleasure. And, as Charlie rode on, the ground slipped away beneath him, and it was as though he and the horse had melted into one.

16

A NEW ADDITION

"Charlie, Charlie, wake up."

Charlie rubbed his hand over his face and looked up to find Nick standing over him.

"Where am I?" he asked, feeling strangely disorientated as he struggled to open his eyes. He looked from side to side, and then he saw that he was in the hospital, and suddenly he remembered everything.

"How did you get here so quickly?" Charlie asked.

"Not so quickly," Nick laughed. "It took me three hours. You've been asleep."

"Have I?" Charlie looked puzzled. "I suppose I must have. I phoned you, then I went and sat down, and then..."

"You must have dropped off," Nick said, squeezing

his shoulder. "It's been a long and exhausting night for you – especially as you rode again. I don't know quite what to say – except that if you hadn't... if you hadn't acted so quickly, well I don't like to think what would have happened. I might not be a proud father for one."

"What?" Charlie sat up quickly. "The baby's born?" Nick grinned.

"Well go on," Charlie said, excitedly. "Don't keep me in suspense. Spill the beans. What is it?"

"A girl," Nick grinned. "A healthy little girl."

"Great!" Charlie cried. "That's fantastic. Doubly fantastic – I've won the bet too."

"Bet? What bet?" Nick looked puzzled.

"I bet Tom it would be a girl." Charlie smirked.

Nick patted him on the back and laughed. "Come on, let's go and see them, and then I'm afraid it'll have to be back to Sandy Lane. Work as usual for us." Nick sighed, but Charlie had never seen him look so happy.

And so the two of them hurried off down the corridor to Sarah's room. Just as they were about to knock and go in, Nick stopped Charlie.

"Before I forget, there's something I need to tell you," he said, seriously. "I might not have the opportunity to catch you on your own over the next few days. It's about that racehorse, Night Star."

Charlie stood very still as Nick went on.

"I phoned the Elmwood Racing Stables from the course," Nick started.

"And?" Charlie asked, his eyes widening with fear.

"And it's all right, Charlie," Nick started. "If you can ever call the death of a horse all right. Night Star died of a heart attack. I hope you don't mind, but I told Josh Wiley what you'd been going through. You see, he was a bit cross that you hadn't been turning up. He couldn't believe it when I told him you thought it was your fault. Anyway, it's all been sorted. Josh is as anxious as I am to work out a training programme for you, although that's by the by now you're riding again." Nick grinned.

"Nick, I–" Charlie didn't know what to say.

"The vet's report came through last week," Nick started again. "The horse had a very weak heart – it could have happened at any time. It's very sad, but it certainly wasn't anything you did. In the nicest way possible, it was the best place for a horse to die – out on the gallops. Now," Nick said, "I think I can hear a baby crying. And you need to put this behind you."

Charlie looked uncertain at first, and then he found his voice. "You're right Nick," he said. "And thanks."

The two of them pushed open the door to find Sarah sitting up in bed holding the latest addition to Sandy Lane.

17

BACK AT THE YARD

Charlie sat tight to the saddle and cantered neatly around the outdoor school.

"Very good," Nick called. "I'm glad those few weeks off haven't made you forget how to ride."

"How could I ever forget that?" Charlie shouted back across the school. He and Nick had returned to the stables that morning to feed the horses, and Charlie hadn't been able to resist getting back in the saddle. Once he was on a horse, he couldn't imagine how he'd ever thought he might not ride again.

"Once more around the school and then I'll be completely ready for my race training," Charlie shouted.

It had been the first thing Charlie had done when he'd got back from the hospital... got straight on the phone to speak to Josh. And Josh had arranged for him to start riding again the next day. Charlie couldn't believe it had all been so easy. He was almost brimming over with excitement about it.

"Now that the horses are all fed, I think I'll go back to see Sarah in the hospital." Nick's voice disturbed Charlie's thoughts. "I'll be back by lunchtime."

"OK," Charlie answered. "What are you going to do about your dressage course though?" he asked.

"Oh that – that will just have to wait another year. There are more important things to think about now. There's going to be a lot to do, what with the baby coming early, and that stable will need rebuilding. To top it all we've got to get you ready for the August Bank Holiday Show, haven't we? It's only two weekends away. You've got a lot of work to catch up on." Nick chuckled. "Still, we can talk about that another time."

"Sure Nick." Charlie grinned.

Calmly, Charlie circled Napoleon around the school and breezily turned him to the course one more time as Nick hurried off. Soaring through the air, they cleared jump after jump with ease. Charlie was so engrossed in his riding that he didn't notice Tom pull up on his bicycle and stand gawping behind the railings. And then Izzy arrived and drew up alongside him.

"I can't believe it." Izzy's mouthed dropped open. "Whatever got him riding again?" The two friends stood mesmerised at the sidelines. It wasn't until Charlie cleared the last jump and drew to a halt that he noticed his two spectators.

"Charlie... what's happened? How did you... how did you..." Tom was flabbergasted and the questions rolled off his tongue one after the other.

"How did I get riding again? Well," Charlie grinned, "it's a bit of a long story."

"Do Nick and Sarah know about this?" Izzy asked. She didn't know what else to say.

"You could say that – Nick was standing where you both are just a minute ago," Charlie laughed.

"Nick? What's Nick doing back?" Tom demanded. "This is getting madder and madder. What on earth is going on?"

"Well, if you'd give me a chance to get a word in edgeways, I'd tell you," Charlie said, turning Napoleon back to the course. "Don't just stand there gawping. Go and get Chancey and Midnight tacked up so we can go out for a hack, then I'll explain. It's good to see you looking happier, Izzy," he called across to his friend.

"Well, it's good to see you riding again," she grinned. "I suppose I've just had to come to terms with boarding school really. After all, I'll still get home for the odd weekend, and there's the holidays too."

"Good on you," Charlie called back.

"But there's one thing you've got to promise me," she went on.

Charlie looked worried at first, and then he relaxed as Izzy smiled.

"You've got to promise to write and tell me all Midnight's news," she grinned.

Charlie groaned. "Well, you know I'm not too hot on letter writing," he joked. "But I'll give it a shot. Come on, let's get going. Right now all I feel like is a good gallop... oh and by the way." He called back to where Tom was still standing by the railings. "You're on mucking out duties next week."

"Mucking out duties?" Tom looked puzzled.

"Yes," Charlie grinned. "I won our bet – Sarah's had a baby girl!"

A Horse for the Summer by Michelle Bates

The first title in the Sandy Lane Stables series

There was a frantic whinny and the sound of drumming hooves reverberated around the yard as Chancey pranced down the ramp. He was certainly on his toes, but he didn't look like the sleek, well turned-out horse that Tom remembered seeing last season. He was still unclipped and his shabby winter coat was flecked with foam as feverishly he pawed the ground. No one knew what to say...

When Tom is lent a prize-winning show jumper for the summer, things don't turn out quite as he hoped. Chancey is wild and unpredictable and Tom is forced to start training him in secret. But the days of summer are numbered and Chancey isn't Tom's to keep forever. At some point, he will have to give him back...

The Runaway Pony by Susannah Leigh

The second title in the Sandy Lane Stables series

Angry shouting and the crunch of hooves on gravel made Jess spin around sharply. Careering towards her, wild-eyed with fear and long tail flying behind, was a palomino pony. It was completely out of control. Jess's heart began to pound and her breath came in sharp gasps, but almost without thinking she held out her arms...

When the riderless palomino pony clatters into the yard, no one is more surprised than Jess. Hot on the pony's hooves comes a man waving a head collar. Jess helps him catch the pony and sends them on their way. Little is she to know what far-reaching consequences her simple actions will have...

Strangers at the Stables by Michelle Bates

The third title in the Sandy Lane Stables series

...Thoughts jostled around in Rosie's mind as she crossed the yard. She couldn't believe how many things had gone wrong in the couple of weeks Nick and Sarah had been gone. She needed time to think. There was something worrying her, right at the back of her mind... something that held the key to it all. But what was it?

When the owners of Sandy Lane are called away, everyone still expects the stables to run smoothly in their absence. No one is quite prepared for all the things that happen over the next few weeks. There isn't time to get help, the children of Sandy Lane have to act fast, if they want to save their stables...

The Midnight Horse by Michelle Bates

The fourth title in the Sandy Lane Stables series

The horse cantered gracefully around the paddock in long easy strides, his tail held high, the crest of his neck arched. His jet-black coat contrasted sharply with the white frost, his hooves hardly seemed to touch the ground as he danced forward.

Riding at the Hawthorn Horse Trials is all that Kate has dreamed of and this year she's in with a real chance of winning. As she works hard to prepare for the day, it seems nothing will distract her from her goal. But then the mysterious midnight horse rides into Kate's life, and suddenly everything changes...

Dream Pony by Susannah Leigh

The fifth title in the Sandy Lane Stables series

The palomino was now just about on their tails. Jess could see that the ponies were lathered with sweat. As they passed, a blonde-haired girl shot Jess and Rosie a look which clearly indicated she considered them to be inferior. Then she dug her heels into her horse's side and galloped away.

"Come on you lot," said Tom. "Let's go. I've seen all I want to of that crazy bunch."

Jess Adams loves riding, and she especially loves riding the ponies at Sandy Lane. When the smart Rychester Riding Stables opens its doors down the road, she doesn't imagine for a moment it will make any difference to her. But then something happens to change all that... something that tests Jess's loyalty to the limit...

USBORNE
6
SANDY
LANE
STABLES